The Field of the
Cloth of Gold

Novels
The Restraint of Beasts
All Quiet on the Orient Express
The Scheme for Full Employment
Three to See the King
Explorers of the New Century
The Maintenance of Headway
A Cruel Bird Came to the Nest and Looked In

Stories
Once in a Blue Moon
Only When the Sun Shines Brightly
Screwtop Thompson and Other Tales

The Field of the Cloth of Gold

MAGNUS MILLS

B L O O M S B U R Y
NEW YORK • LONDON • OXFORD • NEW DELHI • SYDNEY

Bloomsbury USA
An imprint of Bloomsbury Publishing Plc

1385 Broadway
New York
NY 10018
USA

50 Bedford Square
London
WC1B 3DP
UK

www.bloomsbury.com

BLOOMSBURY and the Diana logo are trademarks of Bloomsbury Publishing Plc

First published in Great Britain 2016
First U.S. edition 2016

ISBN: HB: 978-1-63286-286-0
ePub: 978-1-63286-287-7

Library of Congress Cataloging-in-Publication Data is available.

2 4 6 8 10 9 7 5 3 1

Typeset by Hewer Text UK Ltd, Edinburgh
Printed and bound in the U.S.A. by Berryville Graphics Inc., Berryville, Virginia

To find out more about our authors and books visit www.bloomsbury.com. Here you will find extracts,
author interviews, details of forthcoming events, and the option to sign up for our newsletters.

Bloomsbury books may be purchased for business or promotional use. For information on bulk purchases
please contact Macmillan Corporate and Premium Sales Department at specialmarkets@macmillan.com.

For Sue

After a week or so they sent round a message saying they had a surplus of milk pudding. They said they were willing to share it with the rest of us if we went into their camp at noon. All they asked was that we brought our own spoons and dishes. The offer was undoubtedly generous, but we thought the tone of the message was rather curt. Apparently there'd been some kind of blunder. From what we could gather, the blame for the surplus lay squarely with their cooks: it seemed they'd measured the ingredients in the wrong quantities.

'What on earth do they need cooks for?' said Isabella. 'Can't they do their own cooking?'

She'd been complaining about the newcomers for days, and now she had grounds for further criticism.

'I don't know for sure,' I said, 'but I imagine it's just a matter of organization. There's a fair few of them, so they probably find it better to share the jobs around.

It's called division of labour. Some act as porters, some take care of the tents, some wash the clothes, some do the cooking.'

'Some do nothing,' said Isabella.

'Yes, I noticed that.'

'Apart from giving orders.'

'Perhaps the orders are a necessary element,' I said, 'to keep the camp running smoothly. You have to admit it all looks highly efficient.'

'Well, if it's so efficient,' Isabella demanded, 'why did they end up with a surplus of milk pudding?'

This was a good question. An error of such proportions was certainly out of character. Ever since they'd arrived their every move had appeared part of a carefully planned operation. We'd watched them cross the river from the south, bringing with them all manner of equipment, supplies and baggage. Teams of porters travelled back and forth in synchronized relays; accordingly there were no wasted journeys or misplaced items. Evidently they'd selected their ground in advance. We marvelled at the way they deployed their tents in a perfect grid formation. All the pitches were marked out precisely. Each tent was identical in size, colour and shape; each faced in the same direction; and each was separated from the next by exactly the same interval. Several command tents stood slightly apart from the main group. Between them ran a parallel thoroughfare which we'd already nicknamed the 'high street' because it was so busy with uniformed people coming and going. Every tent had a white pennant flying from its peak. When the work was finished the new encampment dominated the entire south-eastern part of the field. Along its boundary ran a low picket fence, and at each corner stood a flagpole. The camp had come into existence during the course of a single day, the process being overseen by a surveyor, a quartermaster and an inspector of works. Their logistical proficiency was astonishing to behold, yet despite all this they'd managed to produce a surplus of milk pudding.

'An unfortunate lapse,' I remarked.

Isabella gazed at the faraway tents; then she said, 'I suppose you're going to accept their offer.'

'Yes,' I replied. 'Aren't you?'

'No.'

'Why not?'

'Because they're rude!' she snapped. 'They constantly ignore us, and they haven't even bothered to come and introduce themselves formally.'

I could have mentioned to Isabella that she was equally guilty of that charge; actually, none of us had made the slightest effort to welcome the new arrivals. Instead we'd all remained aloof, observing them as they went about their task but never drawing near. As a consequence, and because there were more of them than us, we'd suddenly become the outsiders dwelling on the fringes. Now they'd made a gesture of hospitality, and Isabella was determined to reject it. As for going and formally introducing herself, well that was quite beneath her. However, I knew from past experience that there was no point in arguing with Isabella.

'Have you spoken to the others?' I asked.

'Yes,' she said. 'They're going to give it a miss.'

'Presumably Hen won't be interested?'

'I'm sure he won't.'

'So that leaves just me,' I said. 'A lone ambassador.'

'I expect you'll be alright,' said Isabella. 'It's almost noon, so you'd better run along to the feast.'

I glanced over to Hen's tent. There was no sign of him, and I guessed he hadn't been informed of the offer. I would have liked to let him know, but it was too late now. I checked my appearance to ensure I was tidy; then I headed off towards the south-east corner, feeling as I went that the eyes of the whole field were upon me.

It was a bright, blustery day, and the flags were flying. As I approached the outer row of tents I realized I hadn't trodden this stretch of land for a long, long while. The grass grew thick and lush beneath my feet, and I remembered how attractive this area had looked when I first saw it. On close inspection the tents turned out to be surprisingly small. They were buff-coloured and plainly utilitarian, with a single pole and a canopy rising to a point. The comfort of the occupants had patently not been taken into consideration. Even so, the fabric looked sturdy enough to resist the harshest of weather. The command tents were of the same design but much larger, and one of these served as a cookhouse. I had just paused outside it, uncertain of the correct protocol, when an abrupt blast from a trumpet signalled noon. (This trumpet was prominent on Isabella's list of complaints: it sounded daily at dawn, noon and dusk, and never failed to irritate her. Isabella preferred to get up at least three hours after sunrise; if her sleep was interrupted it put her in a bad mood for most of the day. Personally, I quite liked to hear the trumpet's distant tones through the soft walls of my tent, but at short range even I had to confess it was a bit too loud. In fact, it made me jump.) All at once people began to converge on the cookhouse. A flap parted and a man appeared who I recognized as the messenger. With a wave of his hand he summoned me inside.

'Excellent,' he said. 'You've brought your dish and spoon. I'll put you at the front of the queue.'

There were already several people lining up at a counter, but he led me straight past them and presented me to the cooks.

'Make sure he has a generous helping,' he ordered, before slipping away.

I thought the cooks looked a little disconsolate. There were three of them, and they each wore a white cook's hat. They stood behind some large cast-iron vessels, stirring the contents sullenly.

'Hot or cold?' said one of them.

It was a question I hadn't been expecting. To tell the

truth I'd never sampled milk pudding, so I wasn't sure which to choose.

'What do you recommend?' I enquired.

'It's a chilly day for the time of year,' he said, 'so I suggest you try hot.'

'Alright,' I said. 'Hot. Thank you.'

'Sour milk or plain?'

'Don't know.'

'Try plain.'

'Alright.'

'Do you want it sweetened or salted?'

'Sweetened please.'

'Right you are.'

He peered at my dish and I held it out; then, unceremoniously, I received a large dollop of milk pudding. I thanked the cooks and turned away just as the messenger came back. He seemed slightly harassed.

'Where are your companions?' he asked. 'I've been looking out for them but they haven't arrived yet. I hope they won't be much longer.'

'Oh,' I said. 'No, sorry, it's only me I'm afraid.'

The expression that crossed his face was a mixture of consternation and sheer puzzlement.

'We have a surplus,' he said. 'Didn't we make it clear?'

'Yes,' I replied, trying my best to be tactful, 'but I'm the only one who likes milk pudding.'

'Really?' The messenger thought for a moment. 'No doubt Aldebaran will want a word with you.'

He indicated some nearby trestle tables, then left me to enjoy my pudding. I found a place and sat down. The other diners were friendly enough, although they didn't make conversation; not in my presence anyway. The tent creaked and shuddered as the breeze freshened.

After a while I became aware of somebody standing over me. I looked up. It was one of the men I'd seen giving orders when the camp was being established. He didn't announce himself, but I guessed this was Aldebaran.

'Please,' he said, 'finish your pudding.'

I nodded obediently, and he took the seat opposite mine. A few minutes passed in silence: not until my dish was empty did he speak again. 'I understand your comrades won't be joining us?'

'No,' I said. 'Sorry.'

'That's alright,' he said. 'All the more for you. You can come back tomorrow, and the next day, and the day after that if you wish. We want to use up all the pudding before we make any more.'

'Thank you,' I said. 'It's very nice. Very nourishing.'

Aldebaran inclined his head as if my words of gratitude were completely unnecessary. There was, however, another question.

'The woman who swims in the river,' he said. 'Do you know her?'

'Of course,' I replied. 'Her name's Isabella.'

'Ah, yes, Isabella. We've heard about her.'

'She owns the crimson tent,' I added, 'over in the east.'

'She swims every day, does she?'

'Yes,' I said. 'Usually in the morning.'

'I see.'

Aldebaran glanced at the cooks. They were still standing behind their counter, serving milk pudding to latecomers.

'Isabella,' he repeated to himself. 'I wonder if she's the reason?'

He drummed his fingers on the table. I happened to look down, and in the same instant I realized that my spoon and dish were gone. They must have been tidied away during our conversation. When I mentioned this to Aldebaran he told me not to worry.

'Let the cooks take care of them,' he said. 'It'll help keep their minds on the job: they've had too many distractions lately.'

He rose from his seat, gave me a polite nod, and prepared to leave.

'Come back tomorrow at noon,' he said, 'if you wish.'

Once he'd departed I thanked the cooks again, then went outside. The idea had occurred to me that I didn't necessarily have to return the same route I'd come. I decided instead to stroll down the 'high street', between the rows of tents, until I reached the river. Nobody objected, apparently, so I continued on my way. The breeze was still rising and all the flags were at full stretch: it was a pronounced change from the sultry conditions we'd become accustomed to of late. Actually, when I thought about it, life over the recent weeks had been extraordinarily sedate. A succession of warm and languorous days had drifted by, one after another, while we lounged in idle contentment. We'd done nothing of any use, really, except watch the summer go rolling slowly past. We were a handful of tents scattered far and wide across the immensity of the field. All around us was spaciousness, peace and tranquillity.

Now, suddenly, everything was different. We'd been roused from our indolence by the newcomers with their orderly regime, their functional tents and their tireless trumpet blasts.

The person least affected by these developments was Hen. He occupied the extreme western margins, and remained somewhat isolated from the field in general. The incursion in the south-east was of scant interest to him; indeed, when the new tents started appearing he pretended not to even notice. He just carried on attending to his daily affairs as if nothing had altered. Similarly, when the message came round about the milk pudding he kept a markedly low profile. This was typical of Hen. It didn't mean he was being unsociable; merely that his prime concerns were directed elsewhere.

The Great Field, as it was properly known, lay in the bend of a broad, meandering river. Irregular in shape, it was bounded in the east, south and west by water, and in the north it dwindled gradually into wilderness. As far as I knew it had never been cultivated: it was grass-land, pure and simple. To many eyes the field probably looked insignificant; after all, there was nothing to distinguish it from the countless neighbouring fields. For a select few, however, it was the chosen field: the place where momentous events would unfold and come to fruition. I wasn't there by chance, and I presumed neither was Hen.

I originally met him in early spring. By then he'd already been alone in the west for a long, long time. He'd withstood wind, hail and rain with nobody to share his hardship; he'd witnessed indescribable sunsets which could never be repeated; and he'd seen threatening skies which would seldom be outmatched. Yet he regarded these happenings as little more than sideshows. The only thing that mattered to Hen was that he'd reached the field before the rest of us. He told me as much on the day I arrived. I was resting after an arduous journey when he came over and introduced himself.

'I am called Hen,' he said. 'I have a tent in the west, and I was here first.'

'Seen anyone else?' I asked.

'No,' he replied. 'There's only me.'

Obviously, I had no reason to doubt him. One glance across the field assured me it was entirely unpopulated, and I was fully prepared to accept Hen's word that he was the first and only resident. Yet, seemingly, he felt obliged to qualify his statement further.

'Oh,' he added, 'there may be others who claim priority on the basis of some fleeting visit in the dim and distant past. Perhaps they'll return one of these days, perhaps not, but the fact remains that I was the first to settle, which means I have precedence, not them.'

Having made his case, Hen fell silent and stood gazing into the encroaching gloom. I had no idea who he was referring to exactly, but I didn't bother pursuing the subject. I was in a hurry to get my tent pitched before dark. Spring had barely begun and the days were comparatively short, so I needed to get moving quickly. On the face of it, this didn't present any difficulty. The field was truly vast, and my choice of ground was unlimited. Without hesitation I aimed for the lush pastures of the south-east, which in those days lay completely untouched. When I drew nearer, however, I realized why the grass grew so thick and luxuriant: the land in this quarter was soaking wet underfoot. Plainly the south-east was unsuitable, at least for the time being. I'd been wondering why Hen had planted himself so far over in the west. Now I had a partial explanation.

Eventually I selected a temporary plot about halfway across the field. It would suffice until the weather dried up a little, although change was unlikely in the immediate future. Rain continued to fall for nearly a week. Hen and I maintained a polite distance from one another, enduring sporadic downpours privately in the shelter of our separate tents; then, at last, the sun appeared, and the prospects started to improve. The river sparkled under a clear, blue sky; along its banks, the reeds and bulrushes waved in a balmy breeze. The field was flourishing, and I eagerly awaited the halcyon days which I was certain lay just ahead.

Hen's outlook was rather more restrained.

'Halcyon days only occur in the past,' he said. 'They can't be prophesied.'

Despite his sombre manner, Hen could be perfectly agreeable company, and I liked to think he saw me in a similar light. It was clear from the beginning that he preferred to stay mostly in the west. He rarely ventured into the other parts of the field, but his knowledge of our surroundings was second to none. It was Hen, for example, who pointed out that the field had a slope.

'Oh, it's hardly anything,' he said. 'Barely perceptible, but it's there alright: a gradual declivity from north to south.'

I had to admit it was something I'd been unaware of. In fact, only by squinting across the field at ground level was I able to detect any sign of this slope, so gentle was its character. Later, out of sheer curiosity, I took a stroll to the far north. When finally I turned and looked southward, I had a definite feeling of being slightly higher up than when I started. Hen was proved to be quite correct.

Actually, I found it interesting to see the field laid out before me like this. Situated within the bend of the river, it was effectively separated from all the adjacent fields. The wilderness in the north acted as an additional boundary, and together these factors created a distinct sense of seclusion. It was as if our field had been deliberately set aside in order to fulfil some exalted purpose. No wonder we thought of it as somewhere special: the place where momentous events would unfold and come to fruition.

I noticed, however, that the quality of the grass deteriorated the further up the field I progressed. Throughout the north it was coarse and dry, a striking contrast with the verdant south, and presumably a direct consequence of the slope. The land drained from north to south, which meant that the south received more than its fair share of rainwater. Viewed from a northern perspective, this seemed like an injustice.

With these thoughts in mind I wandered down into the south-east. I still harboured the intention of moving there in due course, and I wanted to know if the ground had begun to dry out. I had my eye on a luscious spot within easy reach of the river, and which looked particularly attractive today with the sun shining brightly; yet when I approached I discovered somebody else had beaten me to it. A faint impression in the grass told me another tent had been there until fairly recently. It was already starting to fade but the evidence was unmistakable: I estimated it would take another week before it vanished altogether. In the meantime there was no question of pitching my tent in the same location, so with disappointment I postponed my plans once again.

The remarkable thing about this other tent, though, was its shape: closer examination revealed that the impression in the grass was a perfect octagon. I tried to picture an octagonal tent standing all alone in the south-east, and suddenly I felt a surge of indignation rising up inside me. Having to relinquish the prime position was tiresome enough, but the idea of losing it to some interloper with a fancy, octagonal tent verged on outrageous!

These sentiments were hardly lessened when I considered the practical shortcomings of such a tent. Surely, I reasoned, it would be entirely unsuited to all but the mildest of weather conditions: if it didn't collapse under its own weight, then no doubt it would be blown away at the first hint of a storm. The field, after all, could be a harsh billet at the turn of the season. What it required was a robust, low tent of the kind favoured by frontiersmen. Stout canvas would be the fabric of choice. The octagonal tent, by contrast, was most likely fashioned from an untested cloth chosen more for its appearance than its durability. Perhaps, of course, this was the very reason it was no longer in place: maybe its owners had realized their folly, and retreated to more temperate climes. If so, then they were plainly ignorant of the field's importance; otherwise they wouldn't have abandoned it quite so readily.

As I pondered these arguments it struck me that my feelings on the subject were both contrary and illogical.

In one instant I'd conjured up an imaginary tent, passed judgement on it and wished it out of existence. In other words, I was displaying all the symptoms of acute envy. Somewhere at the back of my mind I knew I was profoundly jealous of the octagonal tent. Without question it must have been a magnificent sight as it stood overlooking the river, and, to tell the truth, part of me regretted never seeing it.

Nonetheless, I was cross with Hen for failing to mention the other tent. If I'd known about it earlier I could have made alternative plans; instead of which, I'd spent a futile fortnight waiting to move to the south-east. It was alright for Hen: he was fully established in the field, whereas my base was merely temporary. I was finding it all rather frustrating. Hen's silence was utterly unfathomable, yet there was nothing to be gained from falling out with him. So I decided for the moment simply to let the matter lie.

The following morning I awoke early and peered out of my doorway. The sun had barely risen, but to my surprise I spotted Hen patrolling the south-east corner of the field. He hardly ever strayed from his western redoubt, so I wondered what could have tempted him so far. Initially I assumed he was taking a stroll by the river, and that he'd roamed a little further than he intended. After a while, however, I noticed he was inspecting the ground beneath his feet. All at once his purpose became clear: he was studying the impression in the grass. He walked round and round it, bobbing down now and again to get a closer look, and appeared totally preoccupied. For several minutes I observed him with interest, then abruptly he turned and came striding back towards the west. I closed my doorway, and reflected on what I'd seen. The explanation for Hen's early-morning foray now seemed obvious. His claim to be the first in the field was directly undermined by the impression in the grass; accordingly, the sooner it faded from sight the better. I knew for a fact that it hadn't faded, not properly, and so for the present he was destined to be disappointed. I had no idea, of course, if he'd ever laid eyes on the octagonal tent; perhaps he only had a mental picture, just as I did. What was certain was that we had a common desire: for different reasons, both of us wanted all traces of the other tent erased for good; then, maybe, normal life could be resumed.

Judging by Hen's behaviour, he was rapidly running out of patience. The next afternoon he made yet another trip to the south-east. This time he approached his objective from an oblique angle. After a long excursion he went ambling down the field from the north, paused casually to inspect the ground, then continued on his way. He must have known that I could see his every move, and plainly he was trying to disguise his actions. He needn't have bothered really, but I had no wish to cause an upset so I willingly played along with the pretence: when next we spoke I carefully avoided any reference to his jaunts in the south-east.

In any case, I had a feeling that the question of the other tent would resolve itself naturally in due course. The weather continued to improve, and in consequence the grass was thriving. My own tent was already nestling in a soft bed of greenery which thickened visibly by the day, and it was the same story across the whole field. A similar notion must have occurred to Hen. As the grass grew his restlessness diminished in proportion until, at last, he ceased his wanderings. Hen's precious claim was finally safe from scrutiny. Now it was my turn to be impatient. Another slothful week had gone by, and inertia was beginning to set in. Tomorrow, I decided, I would definitely make my move.

Unusually for me, I didn't sleep well that night. Possibly it was the humid conditions keeping me awake, but more likely it was the jumbled dreams which always come with upheaval. Either way, I drifted in and out of my slumbers until the small hours; then, sometime around dawn, I became aware of men's voices passing close by my tent. They were fairly indistinct at first, but slowly my ears attuned, and I recognized Hen's formal tones.

'By the way,' he said, 'I am called Hen, and I have a tent in the west.'

'Been here long?' enquired a second voice. It was deep and resonant.

'Quite a while,' said Hen.

'Whose tent is this?'

'He's a newcomer,' Hen replied. 'Just recently arrived.'

'Otherwise you've been all alone?'

'Yes.'

Now the voices began to fade. Evidently, the two of them were moving away towards the river. The conversation dwindled gradually into nothing, accompanied by the receding tramp of feet. After that I lay for a long time dwelling on what I'd heard. Understandably I was a little dismayed at being described as a newcomer, especially by Hen, whom I'd always thought regarded me as a fellow pioneer. Clearly I'd been deluding myself.

There was something else, though, which was rather bewildering. Even in my drowsiness I'd perceived a certain reticence in Hen's words. During the brief exchange he'd made no mention of his perennial claim to be the first in the field, and vaguely I pondered the cause of this omission.

I wasn't sure how long I slept after that. When next I awoke my tent was bathed in warm sunshine. The voices I'd heard all those hours ago were like a distant memory; then, as the light came filtering in, I recalled my resolution of the day before. I was due to make a move, so I got up and looked out across the field. To my absolute astonishment I saw a new tent in the south-east. It was pure white, and appeared to be shimmering under the clear morning sky.

After gazing at it with disbelief for several minutes, I finally roused myself and ventured outside. All was quiet. There was no sign of Hen, or anyone else for that matter, and an air of undisturbed calm lay over the entire field. I paused again to contemplate the scene before me. For reasons which I couldn't explain, the new tent seemed completely familiar, as though it had been standing in the same place for ever. At the same time I felt that it was somehow unapproachable; that henceforward the land it occupied would be out-of-bounds to me. Needless to say, I swiftly dismissed these preposterous notions: what nonsense, I thought; after all, it's only a tent, nothing more than the product of human invention; then I set off towards the south-east to get a proper look.

I had to admit it was a splendid sight; the outline of the new tent was almost classical in its perfection. Its walls were quite steep, with an upper rim surmounted by a decorative mantle. The canopy was made from some white fabric which I couldn't identify, and which gleamed softly in the sunlight. Beneath a curved awning hung an elaborate cloth doorway. Apparently the structure was supported by a single centre pole and a multitude of guy ropes. From its pinnacle flew a distinctive black-and-white pennant, but the tent's most notable characteristic was its shape. Keeping my distance I walked around it in a large circle, counting its many sides. There were eight in total, a fact that confirmed what I already suspected: evidently the octagonal tent had returned.

All of a sudden the doorway parted, and a bearded man

emerged. He was dressed in flowing white robes. I knew that he couldn't have failed to see me standing there: I was barely a stone's throw away, and actually our eyes met for a moment as he surveyed his surroundings. I waited for a nod of acknowledgement, which was customary in such circumstances, but to my surprise he turned and began closing up his tent. Next there followed a prolonged interlude during which he appeared to do nothing in particular, while constantly ignoring my presence; then eventually he moved off towards the river. Naturally, I was dumbfounded: the newcomer had effectively rebuffed me at a glance. I watched in silence as he neared the river bank. Finally, after a further delay, he entered the water and started wading across to the opposite side. His chosen point of departure was in the extreme south of the field where the river was conspicuously broad and shallow. I'd noticed on previous occasions that the sandy riverbed was clearly visible, but the idea of it being a possible crossing place had never occurred to me. This I found slightly annoying. The man's progress was seemingly unhindered by his white robes; they swirled around him as he pressed on towards his presumed destination at the far side of the river. When he reached it, however, he didn't stop; instead, he continued southwards overland before ultimately disappearing from view.

'What do you make of that?' said a voice beside me. It belonged to Hen, who had now resurfaced from wherever he'd been lurking.

'Unbelievable,' I replied.

I thought Hen was referring to the other man's inexcusable conduct, but I was mistaken. With obvious bewilderment he peered at me, then at the river, then back at me again.

'Sorry,' I said at length. 'What do I make of what?'

'The crossing,' said Hen. 'I never knew it was feasible.'

'Oh,' I murmured. 'No, nor did I.'

'I'd always imagined it would be fraught with difficulty, yet Thomas made it look quite straightforward.'

The way Hen uttered the word 'Thomas' seemed to imply that I should instantly recognize the name; that its owner should be well known to me; and, moreover, that I should always have known him. As a matter of fact, I could easily hazard a guess who Thomas was. Even so, it was odd to hear Hen talking like this; it was almost as if he was in awe of the newcomer.

I nodded towards the river.

'Thinking of going across, are you?' I asked.

'No,' said Hen, 'I probably won't bother.'

'Alright,' I said. 'Well, at least let's have a closer look.'

We strode down to the water's edge. The soft sand was indented with recent footprints: these were the only signs that anyone had ever been there, but I sensed they heralded the beginning of a change. There was no bridge; there weren't even stepping stones; yet the existence of a known crossing place was sure to attract others to the field. Whether this presaged good or ill was far less certain. Only time would tell.

Meanwhile, the river glided quietly past. Hen, I noticed, was gazing abstractedly into the distance.

I half-expected our next port of call to be the southeast. I could picture an enjoyable ten minutes as the two of us subjected the octagonal tent to a detailed evaluation: comparing architectural notes; criticising the features we didn't like; and reluctantly granting our seal of approval. I saw this as a harmless pastime; therefore, I was mildly surprised when Hen declined to join in.

'No,' he said. 'I think I'll be getting back to the west if you don't mind. It's where I belong really.'

'You can't be persuaded then?'

'I'm afraid not. Sorry.'

He wished me luck and retreated westward.

Without Hen's involvement the exercise seemed rather pointless, but I headed for the other tent just for the sake of it. I soon realized, however, that I was hardly in a position to offer a serious assessment. My own tent was no more than a basic pyramid with a pole in the middle, wholly unlike the palatial edifice which stood before me. As I studied the ornately embroidered seams, the intricately spliced guy ropes and the elegantly draped contours, I had to confess I could find no fault at all; on the contrary I was full of admiration. Whether there was a need for such extravagance posed a different question altogether.

Equally hard to justify was the sense of trespass that gradually crept over me as I prowled around the newcomer's tent. I had as much right to be in the south-east as anybody else, yet repeatedly I caught myself glancing towards the river on the off-chance he might be coming back. Angered by my own foolishness, I resumed the inspection and did not cease until I was satisfied I'd seen enough; then finally I sauntered away.

As it happened, he didn't return for several days. During this period life went on much as before: the sun shone, the grass burgeoned and I was soon accustomed to the sight of the shimmering white tent. Only one aspect bothered me: undoubtedly the tent looked resplendent in its solitude, but I couldn't help feeling that the owner was acting selfishly. Essentially, the choicest part of the field was being squandered on an empty dwelling, which struck me as unfair. Reserving a place was one thing; prolonged neglect was quite another.

At last, though, he came back. Early one morning I emerged from my tent and saw him strolling around in the south-east. Again he was wearing flowing white robes, and again he failed to acknowledge me. I tried a friendly nod, but it was no use: his self-absorption was patent. Indeed, his entire demeanour suggested his presence in the field had been bestowed by divine gift.

I watched as he approached his tent and began making some adjustment or other. The way he went about it was fascinating to observe: his movements were both unhurried and purposeful in equal measure, as though he had all the time in the world; seemingly every action had to be contemplated in depth before-hand; and he was endlessly pausing for further deliberation. All this I found irritating in the extreme. Why, I wanted to know, couldn't he simply get on with it? He didn't even keep to his own corner: later the same day he came roaming across the field and passed fairly close to my tent, yet he never deigned to look in my direction. Instead, he just walked straight on by as if I didn't exist. Well, I thought, two can play at that game. I decided to have nothing to do with him until he made suitable amends. This, of course, meant my own movements would be severely limited: in effect, I was excluding myself from the whole of the south-east, but it was a cost I was ready to bear.

Over subsequent days the newcomer continued to wander around as though he owned the place. I also observed that he frequently crossed the river and headed southwards into the lands beyond. Sometimes he returned within a few hours; sometimes he didn't. Meanwhile his tent remained unattended. I soon got the impression that he regarded it as a kind of summer retreat, and that his main interests actually lay elsewhere.

I imagined Hen would take a dim view of these relent-less comings and goings. He was, after all, a stalwart of the field who set great store by the fact that he'd been the first to settle. I expected him to be distrustful of the newcomer, but if he was he kept his misgivings very much to himself. One morning I saw the pair of them talking down by the river. To judge by the time they spent together, the subject under discussion must have been highly important; then finally they shook hands and went their separate ways.

F ar off in the north-east, beyond the outermost turn of the river, a flock of birds was wheeling in the sky. They were no larger than specks in the deep blue haze but, nevertheless, there appeared to be a purpose in their behaviour. They looked as if they were following the progress of some object moving slowly through the broad expanse beneath them. I studied the horizon but saw nothing. After a while one of the birds detached itself from its companions and flew due east. The others maintained their whirling vigil, and I wondered what could have enthralled them so much.

Later, during the afternoon, Hen came across to see me.

'What do you make of those birds?' he asked.

'I don't know,' I replied, 'but I've been watching their antics all day and they're slowly getting closer.'

'Really?' he said. 'All day?'

'Yes.'

'I didn't notice them.'

We stood in silence for a long time, gazing at the birds. I sensed, however, that Hen's mind was on other matters.

'By the way,' he said at length, 'Thomas agrees I was the first to settle in the west.'

'Nice of him,' I remarked. 'Is that his name then? Thomas?'

'Of course,' said Hen. 'I told you before.'

'You mentioned him, yes,' I said, 'but he's never come and introduced himself in person.'

Even as I spoke it struck me that I must have sounded very churlish. Here was Hen giving me some news which plainly meant a great deal to him, but my only response was to quibble about some detail. It seemed my resentment of the newcomer was yet to subside, and poor old Hen was on the receiving end. At the same time, I couldn't help noting that his claim had been somewhat diluted from its original form: 'first in the west' was rather different from 'first in the field', and to my ears it was more of a concession than a victory.

I glanced quickly at Hen, realizing I'd probably offended him on several counts, but by now his attention was distracted.

'Look!' he cried, pointing to the north-east.

The birds we'd seen approaching had now reached the far corner of the field where the river made its turn. They'd worked themselves into a frenzy of squawking and flapping of wings, and a few seconds later we saw the cause of their ferment. Below them, drifting on the current, came a boat with a high, curved prow. Reclining in the stern was a lightly clad woman. She had no obvious means of propulsion, and was relying solely on the river to carry her along. When she saw the tents she steered towards the shallows; then she leapt out and dragged the boat into a stand of bulrushes; finally, she carried a number of bundles to the bank before stepping ashore.

Overhead, the birds continued whirling. She waved her arms and shouted at them to go away, but they ignored her. While all this went on, Hen and I had been watching transfixed. Now we debated going over to help.

'I'm not sure she'll need it,' said Hen. 'She looks very independent.'

'We ought to offer,' I said. 'It's the least we can do.'

The woman must have heard us talking because suddenly she peered in our direction. Next moment she was marching towards us, and as she drew near I heard Hen take a deep breath.

'Where is everyone?' she demanded. 'I arrived especially early to reserve a place, but there's nobody here!'

'Apart from us,' I said.

'Obviously apart from you,' she sighed, 'but it's not what I expected at all. I envisaged a vast sea of tents billowing in the breeze, flags flying, pennants fluttering and so forth.'

'Must be a disappointment,' I said.

'Well, it is and it isn't,' she replied. 'To be honest a bit of peace and quiet wouldn't go amiss.'

She looked across at my tent, then at Hen's, then lastly at Thomas's. Its smooth white canopy was glimmering in the afternoon sunlight.

'Whose is that?' she asked.

'It belongs to Thomas,' said Hen. 'He's not here at present.'

'Ah, yes, Thomas,' she said, as though the name stirred some remote memory.

Her eyes lingered on the octagonal tent.

'And you are?' Hen enquired.

'Isabella,' said the woman.

'Pleased to meet you,' he said. 'I am called Hen.'

She looked at him with interest. 'That's an unusual name.'

'It's colloquial,' he said. 'It means "someone who lives in the west".'

'How enchanting.'

She cast him an engaging smile, then turned to me inquisitively. At the same instant a flurry of movement caught my attention.

'Watch out!' I said. 'Your boat's getting away!'

We ran to the river bank. During Isabella's brief absence the birds had descended on the boat and begun pecking at it ferociously. I could now see that it was fabricated entirely from reeds, which must have attracted them. In their excitement they'd managed to dislodge the vessel from its makeshift harbour, and it was drifting rapidly out of reach. All three of us plunged into the water, but it was too late: a swirling eddy seized hold of the boat and whisked it beyond our grasp. Very soon it was floating round the south-east bend of the river, pursued by a frantic whirr of wings.

To my surprise, Isabella was unperturbed by her loss.

'Never mind,' she said, once we'd regained dry land. 'I can easily build another boat.'

'Yes,' I said, 'I suppose so.'

'If things work out here, of course, I won't need to.'

'So you're planning on staying?' said Hen.

'Certainly,' said Isabella.

Her belongings lay nearby, and amongst them I could see a neatly folded tent. There was also an eiderdown (tied with silk cord), a tapestry (wrapped in ticking) and a collection of velvet cushions (loose). She stood for a long while taking in her new surroundings, a dreamy expression on her face.

'Aren't we fortunate,' she said at last, 'to have such a lovely meadow?'

'Actually,' I replied, 'it's properly known as the Great Field.'

The dreamy expression vanished.

'I'm fully aware of that!' she snapped.

'Oh,' I said, 'sorry.'

'Now if you'll excuse me I've got a tent to put up!'

'You don't need any help then?'

'Correct.'

Without further comment, Hen and I made a swift withdrawal. When next we looked back, Isabella had already begun her task. She'd chosen a site at the extreme east of the field, close to the river. Evidently she'd done the job before: she tackled it with speed and efficiency, and seemed to be following a tried and tested routine; then, when everything was in place, she heaved on a slender rope and a beautiful crimson tent rose up from the ground. Within minutes, she had the whole structure securely pegged and guyed.

'Most impressive,' said Hen, as he set off for his own modest quarters.

Isabella's work was far from complete. She now began installing her possessions, and this turned out to be a much slower process. She'd positioned the tent facing west, presumably to catch the sun going down, which meant that her doorway was plainly in my view. I lost count of the number of times she carried those precious items in and out while she decided what went where, and only after constant rearrangement was she eventually satisfied.

Darkness had not yet fallen when Isabella retired for the evening (doubtless in need of a rest after all her exertions). She failed, therefore, to witness Thomas returning across the river. I'd been wondering when he would next grace us with his presence and now, all of a sudden, here he was. I watched intrigued as he came ashore and caught sight of the crimson tent. It looked spectacular in the fiery rays of sunset, and even from a distance I could tell it aroused his interest. Normally, when he arrived back, he swept the field with an all-encompassing glance before switching his attention inward once more: in general he found nothing more engrossing than himself. The crimson tent, by contrast, held his gaze for several seconds. He stood stock still, swathed in his habitual white robes, and gave it a thorough appraisal; then, when presumably he'd seen enough, he continued on his way. A little later I noticed a lamp glowing faintly in the south-east, but it was soon extinguished as he, too, retired for the night.

The following morning was warm and sunny. A promising day lay ahead, and when I looked out I expected to see one or two early-risers making the most of it. Instead I saw nobody, not even Hen. I knew for sure he'd be roving around somewhere in the west, but for the time being he remained outside my line of vision. All I could see were the two faraway tents, one white and one crimson, both with their entrances fastened, and both silent.

An hour passed and the sun climbed higher in the sky, yet still nothing stirred. Personally, I found this incomprehensible: how anyone could sleep so late in the morning was quite beyond me. After a further ten minutes, however, there was movement at last. Isabella emerged from her tent, wrapped in a towel, and tiptoed across the grass to the river bank. She spent a while searching for a suitable spot where it wasn't too steep; then she dropped her towel to the ground and slipped into the water.

Effortlessly, she swam over to the other side, then back to where she started, then back over again. She repeated this exercise a few times before pausing in the shallows. The river rolled quietly on. Isabella lay motionless as the soft morning sunlight dappled the surface; then gradually the current took hold and she was borne downstream. She spread her arms languidly and offered no resistance. There was a bed of reeds at the water's edge, and when she drifted past she must have brushed their stems with her fingertips; all their heads bowed and swayed in a series of gentle ripples. For a brief period she was lost from view behind these reeds, but eventually she reappeared and continued to glide slowly along. She was now approaching the south-east curve of the river and had almost drawn level with the shimmering white tent; at which moment its doorway parted and Thomas stepped out.

He glanced all around, and immediately his eyes alighted on Isabella's recumbent figure. Naturally, under the circumstances, I expected him to show some discretion and pretend not to notice. Instead, I watched astounded as he strode casually to the river bank and engaged her in direct conversation. Obviously I was unable to hear what was being said, but seemingly Isabella was a willing participant in the exchange. She floated idly towards him as they passed the time of day together; then she gave a little laugh and began swimming upstream once more. Thomas strolled in parallel along the grassy bank, his white robes in full flow. When he spotted her discarded towel he picked it up and folded it carefully over his arm; then he stood at the water's edge and waited. In due course Isabella rose from the shallows and he tossed the towel to her. The discussion resumed as she dried herself down. What exactly they found to talk about so soon in their acquaintanceship I didn't know, but he detained her much longer than I would have thought necessary. For her part, Isabella made no attempt to get dressed. Instead she just stayed where she was with the towel wrapped tightly around her. Occasionally she placed her hands on her hips, rocked her head, and swished her hair from side to side, presumably hoping to dry it in the sun's warm rays. Thomas was standing so close to her that the drops of water must have fallen on his bare feet, yet he showed no sign of having felt them. I carried on observing the pair's behaviour for several minutes: it was a fascinating display from both parties, but their performance was about to be interrupted.

S uddenly a sail appeared coming downriver. Isabella took one look at it and vanished inside her tent. Meanwhile, Thomas stared at the approaching boat. A moment later it ran against the bank and a man jumped ashore with a painter in his hand. He held it secure as the boat swung round with the current. Then two other men dropped the sail. They had landed in the extreme north-east corner of the field, and they paused briefly to take stock of their surroundings. I was quite some way away, but even at this distance I could tell they were only making a tentative appraisal. They were gazing over the field and speaking quietly among themselves. All three of them seemed most unassuming. Whether they were planning to stay or merely breaking their journey was unclear, yet a swish of white robes told me that someone had decided to intervene. Thomas went striding along the bank just as the other two men gained dry land; there then followed a rather one-sided exchange during which he addressed them loudly and pointed in various directions, including back up the river to where they'd come from.

The three men stood in a group, facing him but apparently saying little. They had a certain stillness about them which I found admirable, and I was pleased to see that they were standing firm. When Thomas had finished berating them they simply shrugged and remained where they were; then he turned and marched away towards the south-east. When he passed the crimson tent he didn't even glance at it: evidently he'd forgotten about Isabella for the time being.

After a brief conference, the three men dragged their boat onto the grass and began unloading various pieces of baggage and equipment. These included a large tent which they proceeded to erect close by the river. I decided to go and say hello. They looked at me warily as I approached, but I reassured them with a smile and a handshake. The first man was called Hartopp, and he was accompanied by his two sons. I liked them all from the start: I thought they had the bearing of unadorned noblemen.

'I gather you've already met Thomas,' I remarked.

'The fellow in the white robes?' said Hartopp.

'Yes.'

'He didn't introduce himself,' said the younger son, 'but he spoke to us very haughtily.'

'Made us feel most unwelcome,' added Hartopp.

'That comes as no surprise,' I said.

'Thinks he owns the place, does he?'

Clearly Thomas had upset the three of them, but they rose above the slight with dignity and continued pitching their tent. This was a substantial structure: it comprised multiple curves, planes and angles, and appeared to have been designed by an engineer. According to Hartopp it was more than just weatherproof: it was completely storm resistant. He was visibly proud of its innovations, which included an extended awning and a set of pulley blocks for adjusting the guy ropes from within the tent. I was given a concise tour of the interior; then Hartopp opened a trunk and produced a square container made from tin.

'Like a biscuit?' he asked.

'Oh,' I said, 'yes, please.'

He removed the lid and revealed a stash of plain biscuits. We took one each, then went and stood under the awning. My biscuit, I noticed, was imprinted with some numerals.

'It's the date it was baked,' said Hartopp. 'Two years and eleven months ago, to be precise.'

'Very nice,' I said, munching it slowly. 'Tastes quite fresh.'

'Actually,' he explained, 'the word "biscuit" means "twice baked".'

'I didn't know that.'

'The process makes them hard but light, easy to preserve and excellent for sustenance.'

'I see.'

'Which is why biscuits are vital when travelling.'

'Come a long way then, have you?'

'Yes, indeed,' said Hartopp. 'A long, long way.'

While we'd been talking, Isabella had emerged from her tent (fully clothed) and was now pottering around on the river bank. Every now and then she glanced in our direction.

'Do you know Isabella?' I enquired.

'No,' said Hartopp, 'I'm afraid not.'

'She only arrived yesterday,' I said. 'I thought you might have seen her during your journey.'

'Our paths were unlikely to cross,' he replied. 'The river has many tributaries.'

'Really?' I said. 'I never realized.'

At these words Hartopp turned to me. 'You're not from the north-east then?'

'No,' I said. 'In fact, I'm not from the north at all.'

He absorbed this information thoughtfully but said nothing more on the subject. His sons, in the meantime, had finished unloading their boat. It was a sturdy vessel with a rounded hull and looked as if it was built to last. They hoisted the sail again so it could dry properly in the sun before being folded away; then they turned and stood peering upriver.

'Expecting somebody?' I asked.

'Yes,' said Hartopp, 'we have some friends coming, but they seem to have fallen behind.'

Isabella was now standing perfectly still on the bank and gazing into the north-east. Although she was further downstream, she had a better view of the river because of the way it curved. I could tell she'd seen something approaching and, sure enough, a minute later two more boats came in sight. Their crews waved when they saw us. They drew up to the shore and dropped their sails in the same orderly manner as when Hartopp had arrived; then we all manhandled the boats onto dry land. Isabella refrained this time from repeating her dramatic exit; instead, she quietly observed the scene from where she was. Beyond her, in the distant south-east, somebody else was also watching.

The new arrivals (half a dozen in all) were similar in disposition to Hartopp and his sons: they were friendly, courteous and diligent. Their tents, like his, were angular and extensive, and I sensed Hartopp had a proprietorial interest in each of them. Quickly and efficiently they set up camp nearby; when the work was complete they sat down and shared biscuits with one another.

There was a single exception amongst Hartopp's adherents. A man called Brigant had travelled as a passenger in the third boat, and it soon became clear that he wasn't a natural sailor. He staggered ashore looking rather green in the face and headed directly for the middle of the field, as far from the river as possible. He pitched his tent in isolation, then disappeared into its dark confines: we didn't see him again for several days.

The biscuit tin, meanwhile, served as the key to diplomacy. The next morning, Isabella swam and bathed once more in the lower reaches of the river. Again she was intercepted by Thomas, and again he accompanied her along the bank when she returned upstream. He retrieved her towel and they went through the same ritual as before; then the pair of them stood together talking in the sunshine. All this was witnessed by Hartopp and his companions, but to their credit they paid no attention whatsoever: they simply turned their backs until Thomas had gone. At midday, however, as Isabella reposed in the shade of her tent, she was visited by Hartopp's younger son. He took with him an invitation: would she care to come as a guest of the newcomers and join them for biscuits and fruit cordial? In due course Hen and I also received invitations, but Thomas notably didn't.

It was late in the afternoon when I strolled over to the north-east. I went alone. Hen had politely declined the invitation, just as I knew he would, and remained ensconced in his spartan headquarters. When my hosts asked after him I assured them that he wasn't being unsociable; merely that he seldom strayed from the west these days. Their response was magnanimous.

'Never mind,' said Hartopp. 'We'll send him some biscuits as a gesture of our goodwill.'

Half an hour went by while we waited for Isabella, who eventually arrived looking fabulous in crimson. Despite showing up much later than specified, she was treated like minor royalty and given a conducted tour of the new settlement. Afterwards, we all assembled beneath Hartopp's awning. Isabella was fulsome in her praise of the angular tents.

'Very tasteful,' she said. 'Such neat, clean lines; highly refined; absolutely no fuss or clutter.'

'Thank you,' said Hartopp. 'Obviously they're only experimental. Tent design is in constant development.'

'I think you're a bit of a perfectionist,' she remarked.

'Yes,' he said, 'when it comes to tents I suppose I am.'

'Do they require much upkeep?' I asked.

'Ceaseless,' he affirmed.

Immediately, he began making adjustments to one of the guy ropes. We watched him carefully tighten it, then slacken it a little, then tighten it again. Finally, when he was satisfied with the tension, he came and rejoined us.

'Maintenance,' he said, 'is essential.'

'Oh, I'm hopeless at all that,' said Isabella. 'My tent's riddled with imperfection.'

'Looks alright to me,' I said.

'You've only seen it from faraway,' she replied. 'Actually it's a mass of sags and bulges.'

Hartopp furrowed his brow.

'Are your guys equidistant?' he asked.

'More or less,' said Isabella.

'It's fairly important,' he said. 'A small modification can make all the difference.'

'Really?'

'If you like, I can come and see to it for you.'

'Thank you,' she said. 'That would be lovely. Yes, we really must arrange it sometime.'

'Tomorrow?' suggested Hartopp.

Isabella took a moment to consider her answer.

'Probably not just yet,' she said, casting him a winning smile.

The sun was beginning to go down. Biscuits and cordial were served. As the guests mingled, I gazed around the little encampment. Over by the river bank, I noticed, the three boats had been upturned and were resting on wooden blocks. Something told me they'd be there for quite a while.

The following morning I awoke early. I gazed out at the tents ranged far and wide across the field: all around me was spaciousness, peace and tranquillity. Another warm day lay ahead, so I decided to take a walk by the river while it was still relatively cool. This necessarily involved a detour away from the southeast: in spite of recent events my stand-off with Thomas remained unresolved, and I continued to avoid him at all costs. My plan, therefore, was to aim for the extreme south of the field before heading due west. When I neared the water's edge, however, I changed my mind. The lack of rainfall had started to affect the level of the river, and it was especially shallow at the southernmost point. All of a sudden I was taken with the notion of wading over to the other side: it would be interesting, I thought, to see the field from an entirely different angle, and a change of scenery would do me good. I wasn't one of those people who roamed about barefoot, so I removed my boots and carried them with me. The going was easy, and I was soon at the opposite bank. Some footprints in the sand told me this was the spot where Thomas regularly came ashore; today, for the first time, I added some prints of my own. It was beginning to evolve into a proper crossing.

Once I'd reached dry land I turned and looked back at the field. Immediately I was struck by the preponderance of the shimmering white tent; in comparison, my own tent appeared tiny and insignificant, and so did Hen's, while the new tents in the north-east were barely visible through the early-morning haze. Seemingly, Thomas had chosen his ground well. It gave him full command of the river (as well as the best views) and the implication was clear: anyone approaching from the south was bound to assume Thomas was more important than the rest of us. No wonder he strutted around as if he owned the place; indeed, I would hardly have been surprised if he'd demanded tithes from we lower mortals, or maybe levied a toll for using the crossing. As a matter of fact, I suspected Hen was already in Thomas's thrall. The way he'd continually amended his claim to be first in the field suggested they'd come to some kind of feudal agreement. Obviously this was only conjecture on my part, but there was plenty of evidence to support the theory. Whenever I mentioned Thomas's name, for instance, Hen sounded as though he was doffing an imaginary cap. Moreover, he rarely paid visits to the north, the east or the south. In effect, Hen was confined to his western outpost. There were, however, two sides to this particular coin. During the past few weeks I'd never seen Thomas venturing very far into the west: whenever he wandered in that direction he always stopped well short of the margins. Thomas was apparently keeping to his half of the bargain. In consequence, Hen was free to enjoy a solitary existence, which was what he actually preferred. Maybe he was more astute than I thought.

I pondered all this as I continued to roam through the neighbouring lands. I drifted eastward and Isabella's crimson tent came into view. The sun was up, but it was not yet the hour for her daily swim and there was no sign of movement. (Brigant's tent, meanwhile, lay silent and still.)

By now I was starting to feel an odd sense of detachment. I was only separated from the Great Field by the width of the river, but already I felt disconnected from Hen, Isabella and the others. I realized that the field was where I truly belonged, and all at once I was overcome by an urge to go back. I turned and headed for the crossing, which was when I spotted Thomas advancing towards the far side. He was strolling down the river bank in his usual unhurried manner. I had no idea if he'd seen me or not, but it was too late to change my mind now. I entered the water at the same moment as he did, and waded into the shallows. As we got nearer to one another it occurred to me how different we were: I was carrying a pair of boots in my hand and he was wearing flowing white robes. Also, he was bearded whereas I wasn't. We had nothing in common except that we both dwelt in the same field. For some reason he thought he was superior to everybody else, and I expected at least a reprimand for using the crossing without his permission. I was surprised, therefore, when we passed each other and merely exchanged nods. Not a word was spoken, and I was rather nonplussed by the encounter. Whether he'd given me a nod of greeting, acknowledgement or plain condescension remained unclear, but by the time I reached the bank I'd decided it scarcely mattered. I watched Thomas as he retreated slowly and purposefully into the distant south. It was obvious that neither of us were likely to alter our ways in the near future; accordingly, our exchanged nods represented a sort of unspoken accommodation between us. They were nods of mutual acceptance, which was fine by me.

I had to admit this change of perspective was most welcome; in fact, as the morning unfurled I began to feel somewhat uplifted. Presently, Isabella emerged and went bathing in the river uninterrupted. She swam a long way beyond the shimmering white tent, giving it hardly a second glance as she passed it by; afterwards she returned to the shore and spent the rest of the day sunning herself.

During the afternoon I wandered over to see Hartopp. Although they were newcomers to the field, he and his followers seemed to have blended in quite readily. Nothing was too much trouble in the way of hospitality, and they were never-failing in their helpfulness. Hartopp was still awaiting the call to iron out Isabella's imperfections, but as yet it hadn't come. Instead he immersed himself in the study of tents. All problems of design, structure and function, he explained, could be solved on scientific principles.

Meanwhile, his two sons went in search of Isabella's missing boat. The previous evening I'd recounted the events surrounding her arrival, and they'd been intrigued by my description of the errant vessel. Now they were forming a search party. Perhaps, they suggested, the boat had become lodged amongst the reeds at the far south-west turn of the river (they even considered recruiting Hen as a local guide, but then decided they could manage unassisted). I thought the plan was doomed to failure from the start: wherever the boat came to rest, it was sure to have been pecked to pieces by the birds. Nonetheless, the brothers set off eagerly to seek their trophy. Presumably, they hoped to win Isabella's favour when they brought it back in triumph. Disappointment, however, stood in their way. After hours spent scouring the reed beds, they returned empty-handed.

Following this brief swirl of activity, life continued at its former sedate pace. Thomas finally reappeared and resumed his stately residence in the south-east; and once again he set his sights on Isabella. For several successive mornings he joined her at the riverside, carrying her towel and playing the humble attendant. I had to confess I admired his persistence: without question it was a gallant effort, yet she wasn't fooled for a moment. Not Isabella. She may have dried herself in public, but she always dressed in private. Thomas's repeated overtures were getting him nowhere, and ultimately his interest began to wane. As Hartopp could have told him, Isabella was more or less unreachable.

Despite these minor let-downs, there was no real cause for complaint. In truth, we lacked for nothing. Each of us possessed the tent of our choice; we enjoyed luxurious seclusion; and the weather was warm and sunny. We were a handful of settlers scattered far and wide beneath the broad, blue sky. All around us was peace and tranquillity and, as the summer rolled on, a sense of timelessness descended over the field.

It was Brigant, of all people, who alerted us to the intruders. I say 'of all people' because he was the last person I'd have expected to raise the alarm. Generally he minded his own business and kept matters very much to himself. He was the type who noticed a lot but said little in the way of comment. Moreover, he wasn't usually to be found roaming about at the crack of dawn, which was when the advance party made its appearance.

Brigant had taken a while to adapt to his new circumstances. In the days following his undignified arrival he'd remained hidden inside his tent, lost entirely to the world at large and displaying no obvious sign of life. I soon decided that he must be a recluse by choice, but Hartopp had different ideas. He felt responsible for the welfare of his passengers, and gradually Brigant's prolonged torpor became a cause for grave concern. Apparently, his recent history was rather discouraging.

'Brigant was never a good traveller,' Hartopp explained.

'We had to stop the boats on countless occasions during our voyage.'

Hartopp, Isabella and I debated what we should do. In my opinion it was best simply to leave Brigant alone until he'd made a proper recovery, but I was overruled by Isabella.

'We can't just leave him,' she said. 'He looked very peaky when he landed, and he might be even worse now.'

So it was that I found myself in a small deputation heading for Brigant's tent. It stood in the middle of the field and, by default, I was his nearest neighbour (hence my involvement). The tent was an unglamorous affair: a ridge tent, with a wooden knob at the top of each pole. Its canvas walls flapped limply in the wind as we approached. We paused and listened, but heard no sound; then Hartopp spoke quietly.

'Brigant?'

His enquiry brought no response.

'Brigant?'

Again nothing.

'Perhaps he's asleep,' I said.

'Perhaps,' answered Hartopp. 'Even so, it's a bit worrying.'

'I really think we should have come sooner,' said Isabella.

We watched as she leaned in close to the tent.

'Brigant?' she called softly. 'Brigant?'

There was a low groan from within, then a hoarse voice demanded, 'What's all the noise?'

'Oh, hello, Brigant,' said Hartopp. 'We're just seeing if you're alright.'

'I'll survive,' came the reply.

'We've brought you some biscuits.'

I thought I heard the onset of a second groan, but it was quickly suppressed.

Instead, the voice murmured a weak, 'Thank you.'

The three of us waited. From inside the tent there came a further series of groans, faint cursing and exasperated puffing; then, at last, Brigant's gaunt head appeared in the entrance.

'Morning,' he said, to nobody in particular.

'Afternoon actually,' said Isabella.

She was dressed as usual in dazzling crimson, but Brigant seemed unmoved by her splendour.

'I stand corrected,' he said, before emerging fully into the daylight.

'Well,' said Hartopp cheerily. 'Glad to see you out and about.'

He presented Brigant with a tin of biscuits and assured him there were plenty more where they came from.

'Let me know when you need replenishing,' he added.

Brigant was evidently overwhelmed by this act of generosity. He stared speechlessly at the offering while Hartopp went and fussed around the tent, tightening the guy lines and so forth. There was little to adjust, in fact, but the work kept Hartopp busy for a few minutes.

'That's better,' he announced finally.

'Thank you,' uttered Brigant for a second time.

Hartopp smiled, and said he'd better be getting back to the north-east.

After he'd gone, Brigant peered doubtfully at his biscuits.

'Many more of these,' he said at length, 'and I'll go down with scurvy.'

'Oh,' I said, with surprise, 'I think they're quite nice.'

'Maybe they are,' said Brigant, 'but you probably haven't had to live on them for the past year and a half.'

'No,' I replied. 'No, I haven't.'

'Still,' said Isabella, 'it was kind of Hartopp to bring them over.'

'Yes, if you say so,' conceded Brigant in a weary tone. He put his hand to his brow and closed his eyes for several long moments, then he opened them again and focused properly on Isabella.

'And you are?' he asked.

'Isabella.'

'I'm Brigant.'

'Yes, so we heard,' she said. 'Pleased to meet you.'

'Likewise,' said Brigant.

He gave me a nod, then turned and peered at the elegant white tent that shimmered in the distance.

'Alright for some,' he remarked. 'Very posh.'

'It belongs to Thomas,' said Isabella.

'Is that Thomas the Proud?'

'Just Thomas,' she said, 'as far as I know.'

I was beginning to warm towards Brigant, in spite of his rather blunt manner. He looked across to the west, where Hen was busily engaged in some task or other.

'Who's that fellow?' he enquired.

'His name's Hen,' I said. 'He was here first.'

'Really?' said Isabella. 'I thought Thomas was.'

'Is that what he told you?'

'Not in so many words,' she said, 'but I always assumed he was here before anyone else.'

'That's debatable,' I replied. 'In any case, Hen was the first to settle so he has the prior claim.'

'But . . .'

Isabella got no further because she was suddenly interrupted by Brigant.

'Does any of this really matter?' he snapped. 'After all, it's only a blasted field we're talking about!'

I glanced at Brigant with astonishment. Plainly he didn't share my idealistic vision of the field: a place chosen especially to fulfil its purpose; a place where momentous events would unfold and come to fruition. In Brigant's view it was merely a 'blasted field'. During the silence which followed his outburst I wondered if his judgement was possibly correct, and if maybe I'd been deceiving myself from the very start. When I considered the question in any depth, I realized that nothing of significance had happened in all those weeks since my arrival. There'd just been sunshine, rain, and more sunshine, accompanied by a slow trickle of newcomers. The facts were irrefutable: the sparse population was barely enough to put us on the map, let alone stir up great events.

Isabella's expectations had similarly failed to transpire. She'd envisaged a vast sea of tents billowing in the breeze, with flags flying and pennants fluttering aloft. It was a vivid picture, and I could easily imagine the scene she'd painted, but as yet it had come to little.

Nevertheless, she remained optimistic.

'Well, whoever was here first,' she said, 'I think we're all fortunate to have such a lovely meadow.'

Her words seemed to smooth Brigant's ruffles.

'I suppose it'll do,' he said at length.

Brigant may not have been impressed by his new surroundings, but there was one feature that definitely caught his interest.

'I see we've got a bit of a slope,' he observed.

'Oh, yes,' I said. 'It's hardly anything really. Almost imperceptible.'

'A slope's still a slope,' said Brigant.

He looked up the field towards the wilderness in the north, then turned again and gazed south.

'Hmm,' he said thoughtfully. 'Always a good test, a slope is.'

I wasn't sure what he meant by this remark. Over the

next few days, however, he gradually expanded on the subject. In conversation, he began making reference to the 'lower field' and the 'upper field', as though the Great Field was somehow divided into two halves. The slope, apparently, was an integral part of this division. Any land that lay to Brigant's south was the lower field, while the upper field was the land that lay to his north. The line between the two halves was completely arbitrary, of course, yet Brigant persisted in distinguishing one from the other. Furthermore, I noted that he tended always to favour the north. He could often be seen strolling around in the upper field, as he called it, but he seldom ventured southward.

Consequently, I was surprised when early one morning I heard Brigant's voice outside my tent.

'Are you awake?' he asked quietly.

'Only just,' I said. 'What are you doing up and about at this hour?'

'Couldn't sleep,' he replied.

'That makes a change.'

'Can you come out here please?'

I detected a sense of urgency in his tone, so quickly I put on my boots and went outside.

Brigant was peering towards the river.

'What do you make of those characters?' he said.

Over on the other bank were three tents, buff-coloured and conical in shape, with white pennants fluttering from their peaks. Standing beside these tents was a small group of men. They were all clad in identical buff tunics, and all looking in our direction.

'Not sure what to make of them,' I said. 'Any idea how long they've been there?'

'No,' said Brigant. 'I didn't see them arrive.'

'They seem to be sizing us up.'

'That's what I was thinking.'

A movement in the south-east caught my eye. Thomas appeared in the doorway of his tent, and he soon noticed the men on the opposite bank. I expected him instantly to go marching towards them, just as he had when Hartopp and his companions first landed. Instead, though, he stayed where he was, observing the newcomers but, for the time being, doing nothing.

Brigant, meanwhile, withdrew to his northern hideaway.

This was the state of affairs for the rest of the morning. One by one, Hen, Hartopp and the others turned out to greet another day, only to be met by the sight of the three conical tents. Last to emerge was Isabella. The sun had risen quite high when I saw her tiptoe to the water's edge. As usual, she discarded her towel and slipped into the river, swimming a few widths before drifting gently downstream. When she neared the shimmering white tent she paused briefly in the shallows, then headed upriver once again. Isabella completed her daily exercise and came ashore, apparently unaware of developments on the southern bank.

A little later, however, after she'd dressed, I saw her

gazing across at the neighbouring field. She stood for a long while shading her eyes with her hand, as if studying the landscape in detail, then she came and spoke to me.

'I see there are some new arrivals,' she said.

'Yes,' I replied. 'They've been here since early morning.'

'I like their pointy tents.'

'Guessed you might.'

'Don't like the colour though.'

'Ah.'

'Of all the colours in the world, they go and choose buff!' she said with disdain. 'Even their clothes! Honestly, some people have no sense of gaiety.'

'Apart from him,' I remarked.

Isabella knew exactly who I was talking about. One of the men seemed somehow different from his comrades. He was tall in stature and noticeably bronzed, and wore a purple sash over his tunic. I presumed from his deportment that he was their leader: occasionally he strode amongst them dishing out commands, but at present he was standing alone near the river, contemplating the Great Field as it lay spread out before him.

'Yes, well, he is rather exceptional,' said Isabella.

'I think he's a bit of a show-off,' I said, 'parading up and down in that purple sash of his.'

We watched as he rejoined the other men and issued a stream of orders. Immediately they abandoned their posts and vanished inside two of the tents. Their leader waited for a few moments, took a final glance across the river, then retired into the third tent.

'I expect they need some sleep if they've been travelling all night,' I said. 'I imagine they've come a long way.'

'From the far south, I suppose,' said Isabella.

'Yes,' I agreed, 'most probably.'

As the afternoon passed, the newcomers became a source of increasing conjecture among the rest of us. In due course, Hartopp's elder son, Hollis, went down to the crossing to get a closer view of the three tents. On his return, he reported that the fluttering pennants all bore the letter J.

'I wonder what they want?' said Hartopp.

'A place to stay, perhaps,' I suggested.

'Then why don't they cross the river?'

This was a good question. Throughout the evening, muffled conversations could be heard inside various tents as the subject was earnestly pondered. Even Hen came over from the west to join the debate. No conclusions were reached, however, and by the following day nothing had changed.

I arose early and looked southward. The men in the other field were already out and about, but at first I could see no sign of their leader. After a while, though, I spotted him patrolling the river bank in the east. He was more or less opposite Isabella's crimson tent, which he studied briefly from his vantage point before moving on. He treated Hartopp's small encampment to the same cursory examination, then he turned and headed back the way he'd come, pausing only to glance at the shimmering white tent. Thomas, it should be mentioned, had remained aloof during the previous evening's discussions. Hitherto, I'd assumed that the continuing presence of the newcomers would be enough to spur him into action, and indeed Hen had expressed a similar view. After all, it was Thomas who swanked around as if he owned the place, and whose tent dominated the lush pastures of the south-east. Yet he'd done nothing beyond quietly observing the situation from his doorway.

Now, as the bronzed individual passed by on the other side of the river, I wondered who would make the next move.

Isabella, needless to say, was allowing nobody to impinge on her daily routine. Around mid-morning she emerged from her tent, tiptoed to the bank, discarded her towel and slipped into the water. I thought she swam rather more vigorously than usual, and she also spent less time drifting inertly downstream. The cause for this may have been a recent change in the weather: the long sultry period was coming to an end at last. The sun still shone brightly, but a breeze was rising and the temperature had dropped a little. Isabella evidently made up the difference by summoning a burst of energy. Afterwards, when she'd dried and dressed, she came over to see me and Hen. We were standing by my tent, just like the day before, gazing into the south. This was now our main pastime. Ever since the arrival of the newcomers, we'd all become preoccupied with events in the neighbouring field. To tell the truth, we did nothing except watch them while they watched us. Although nobody would admit it, the worst problem was the interminable waiting. With these outsiders seemingly poised to strike across the river at any minute, it was difficult to enjoy the peace and tranquillity to which we were accustomed. Isabella was particularly impatient for the matter to be resolved.

'Come on then, if you're coming,' she murmured, her eyes fixed on the distant sentinels.

'They're certainly biding their time,' remarked Hen. 'Unless, of course, they're undecided about what to do next.'

'Well,' said Isabella, 'I wish they'd make their minds up.'

Suddenly, and for reasons I couldn't explain, I felt impelled to put an end to the deadlock. Without a word to the others I set off towards the crossing, uncertain of exactly what I would do when I got there. The men at the other side saw me approaching, but stayed where they were: obviously they were allowing me to come to them. I was struck by the thought that this could be viewed either as a tactical advantage or a sign of weakness. Either way, there was no turning back now, so I entered the shallows and waded to the opposite bank. As I gained dry land, the man with the purple sash strode forward to meet me.

The opening exchange was polite enough.

'Morning,' he said.

'Morning,' I replied.

'Weather's freshening up.'

'Yes, seems that way.'

'I expect the water's cold.'

'It's not too bad.'

He regarded me in silence for a few moments, then nodded at the shimmering white tent.

'That yours, is it?' he asked.

He knew very well it wasn't mine: he and his subordinates had been spying on the field for the past twenty-four hours, and they knew precisely which was my tent, which was Thomas's and so forth.

'No,' I said. 'It isn't.'

'So who's in charge then?'

'Nobody.'

'Really?' he said. 'That's an odd arrangement.'

'Not for us, it isn't. As a matter of fact, it's perfectly normal.'

'Glad to hear it.'

His tone so far had been conversational, probably in an attempt to put me at my ease.

Now, however, he dispensed with the subtlety.

'Come on then,' he said. 'State your business.'

'Well,' I said, 'some of us who've been here for a while were wondering what your plans might be.'

He gave me a quizzical look. 'What difference does it make how long you've been here?'

'It makes a difference to some,' I assured him.

'I see.' He paused briefly before continuing. 'Our plans,' he said at length, 'depend on what's on offer.'

'Ah.'

'So if you'll spell out your terms we can take it from there.'

'Right.'

I was beginning to realize I'd crossed the river entirely unprepared for this encounter. I had no idea what kind of offer he was referring to, or how it could possibly affect his plans. Moreover, it was becoming clear that I needed to be circumspect in my dealings with these people. I could tell they weren't here just to play games: on the contrary, the outcome of our meeting could be critical.

'Before we start,' I said, 'may I enquire who I'm talking to?'

'I would have assumed you knew that already,' he answered tersely. 'I am Julian.'

'Sorry,' I said. 'Yes, of course.'

I glanced towards the three conical tents, where the other men stood observing the proceedings. From the peak of each tent flew a white pennant, emblazoned with a purple letter J.

Julian, in the meantime, was waiting for my next move.

'So?' he said.

'I'll probably need to consult with the others,' I replied.

'Consult?' he repeated. 'But surely you were sent over to negotiate.'

'Sort of, yes,' I said.

'What do you mean "sort of"?'

Julian's manner was getting increasingly irritable, unfriendly even, and I was at a loss for what to say next without causing further upset. Just then, however, he began peering into the distance.

'Aha,' he said. 'Who's this coming?'

Immediately I turned and saw Thomas entering the river at the far side, his white robes swirling all around him. Julian instantly forgot about me and marched to the water's edge; then he stood stock still, waiting, as Thomas drew near. His followers, meanwhile, watched attentively.

I never thought I'd be pleased to see Thomas wading across the river, but on this occasion I was more than pleased: I was delighted, not to mention thoroughly relieved. Undoubtedly, I'd taken on more than I could handle. All at once, with Thomas riding to my rescue, I felt a great burden being lifted from me.

Nonetheless, there was a price to pay. As Thomas stepped ashore, he shook hands courteously with Julian. The pair then came wandering inland together, deep in conversation. Evidently, Julian had invited Thomas to inspect the three conical tents. The route they took passed within a few yards of where I was standing, yet neither of them granted me so much as a nod. They simply ignored me and continued on their way. Julian's underlings witnessed this blatant snub and openly smirked about it amongst themselves. In response, I turned and stalked off to the river bank. Next minute I was in the shallows and heading back towards the Great Field.

By the time I reached the opposite shore, my mood had subsided into sheer disgruntlement. The episode with Julian had been highly embarrassing, and I was inclined to make directly for my tent and lie low for several days. What I didn't want to face was a reception committee, so when I saw Isabella and Hartopp coming to meet me I quickened my pace. It was no use, though: they cut across and intercepted me before I reached sanctuary.

'What's this?' I demanded. 'A post-mortem?'

Hartopp appeared startled by my harsh words.

'No,' he said, 'we've come to congratulate you.'

'Oh?'

'A brilliant move,' he added.

I stared at him with bewilderment. 'What move?'

'Don't be modest,' said Isabella. 'It was you who set the wheels in motion. You went and parleyed with the newcomers and prepared the ground for Thomas. Excellent work!'

For a few moments I allowed myself to bask in this unexpected praise, then I offered a verdict of my own.

'Well,' I said, 'he'll need to keep his wits about him when he's talking to those people.'

'Why, what are they like?' asked Hartopp.

'I only spoke to Julian,' I replied, 'and he struck me as a rather prickly customer.'

'Is he the one with the purple sash?'

'Correct.'

'He looks very athletic,' said Isabella.

'An apt description,' I said. 'Yes, I imagine he's quite competitive when it comes to the cut and thrust.'

'Still,' said Hartopp, 'they've only got three tents, so we'll most likely manage to find them a place.'

Hartopp was being his usual generous self, but I had a feeling that matters weren't as simple as he thought. Somehow, I couldn't picture the newcomers meekly settling amongst the rest of us. The way they'd surveyed the field from a distance suggested that their intentions were altogether much grander; and Julian's remarks about what might be on offer only underlined my suspicions.

At the other side of the river, Thomas's mission was ongoing. We watched as he was given a guided tour of the conical tents; then he sat down for further discussions with Julian. These lasted an hour or so before the pair of them rose abruptly to their feet and headed for the crossing. Side by side they entered the water and waded towards the Great Field.

'Here they come,' announced Isabella.

I noted with interest that she didn't venture down to greet Julian; neither did Hartopp.

As soon as they stepped ashore, Thomas led his guest to the shimmering white tent, presumably for a reciprocal tour of inspection. Afterwards, Julian spent a good while pacing around in the south-east, gazing in all directions and generally studying the lie of the land. Thomas, in the meantime, stood quietly aside.

Darkness was falling when I saw Julian returning across the river. Isabella and Hartopp had long since drifted back to their tents, both apparently in the belief that the meeting had reached a satisfactory conclusion. I wasn't quite so sure. Over the past few days Thomas seemed to have lost much of his previous strut and swagger. For reasons of his own he'd shouldered the mantle of responsibility, but I was uncertain whether he was a match for Julian.

Unsurprisingly, I had another restless night. In a series of peculiar dreams featuring Isabella, Julian and me, I constantly found myself on the wrong side of the river trying to get across. Sometime after daybreak I woke up all in a tangle and peered out through my doorway. I half-expected Julian's tents to have moved into the Great Field. To my amazement, however, they'd vanished completely, and so had the shimmering white tent.

It took me a few seconds to adjust to this drastic change of scenery. The south-east suddenly appeared forsaken and empty without its prize exhibit overlooking the river, and the surrounding fields had a similar air of abandonment. Beneath a grey, overcast sky, an unseasonably brisk wind came gusting out of the east, doing little to enhance the gloomy prospect. With a mounting sense of disquiet I emerged from my tent and glanced all around.

Thankfully, nobody else had gone: Isabella, Hartopp, Brigant and Hen were still in their usual places.

Actually, Hen was already up and about, and when he saw me he came sauntering over.

'Morning,' he said. 'Quite a change from yesterday.'

'Yes,' I agreed.

'The birds have flown.'

'Did you see them go?'

'Yes, very early,' said Hen. 'They all went off together.'

'Really?'

'Those other people helped Thomas with his tent, then the entire company headed southward.'

Hen's disclosure was most intriguing, and for a while I pondered the information in silence.

Over at the far side of the field we could see Hollis slowly making his way along the river bank, pausing from time to time at the various viewpoints. Keeping a respectful distance, he skirted around Isabella's crimson abode before continuing towards the south-east. When he reached the turn of the river he stopped and peered at the ground. I knew precisely what he was looking at: he was examining the octagonal impression left in the grass by Thomas's tent. Over the past few weeks I'd noticed that Hollis approached most subjects in a forensic manner, a trait which I supposed he'd inherited from Hartopp. He seemed fascinated by everything scientific, mechanical, mathematical and, in this case, geometrical.

Hen, who was still standing beside me, said nothing. Was he tempted, I wondered, to go and see the impression for himself, just to confirm that Thomas had definitely gone?

Hollis, meanwhile, had resumed his journey along the river bank, and was now on the southern stretch. When he neared the crossing he halted for a moment as if contemplating his options, then without further delay he entered the water and waded to the other side. As Hen and I looked on, he went ashore and headed for the spot where the three conical tents had stood. Once again he inspected the ground, closely studying the impression left by Julian and his comrades.

'Did you find out what they wanted?' asked Hen, finally breaking the silence.

'Not really, no,' I replied. 'It was all rather vague.'

'Maybe Thomas found out.'

'Yes, maybe,' I said, 'but we'll probably never know.'

Eventually Hollis turned and retraced his steps back to the north-east. Whether he'd learnt anything from his investigations was unclear, but Hen and I were certainly no wiser than he was. A great unanswered question now hung over the field, a question that would dominate everyone's thoughts and conversations during the succeeding days. Despite endless conjecture, nobody could explain the swift departure of both Thomas and Julian's people.

There was also a secondary matter for consideration, raised largely at the behest of Isabella.

'The field looks completely wrong now,' she announced, one blustery afternoon. 'It's all gone out of balance.'

She was referring to the emptiness of the south-east, her implication being that the vacant space should be taken over by one of us.

'Why don't you move then?' I suggested.

'No, I'm perfectly happy where I am,' she said. 'I actually meant you.'

I could see the logic of her argument. In reality, I was the only candidate. Neither Hartopp nor Brigant showed the slightest inclination to head southward, and I knew that Hen was firmly embedded in the west. The trouble for me, as always, lay with the impression in the grass. Once again I was reluctant to transplant my tent until all traces of the previous occupant had faded away. Therefore, I decided to stay where I was for the present.

'Suit yourself,' said Isabella, 'but you're missing a golden opportunity.'

That night I lay listening to the wind as it gradually increased in strength. Without doubt we were in for a period of inclement weather. I was confident it would improve again sooner or later: there was no reason why it shouldn't. Nevertheless, the halcyon days of summer now felt far removed, and it occurred to me that they'd passed without my even noticing.

Around dawn the clamour of the wind was augmented by another sound which at first I couldn't identify. It was coming from the south, and as I slowly awakened I recognized the distant blast of a trumpet. I looked out through my doorway and saw a huge assembly of men on the other side of the river. They were all clad in buff-coloured tunics, and as I observed them a sort of dull realization crept over me: Julian and his minions were merely the advance party; now, at last, the main body had arrived.

There was nothing to be done, of course. We few settlers were powerless to prevent an influx of such magnitude. Quickly I alerted Hartopp and the others to the situation in the south, then we watched in silence as the newcomers got themselves organized. Within an hour they were swarming across the river, carrying all kinds of equipment, supplies and baggage. Their logistical proficiency was astonishing to behold: it was evident they'd selected their ground beforehand, and every move appeared part of a carefully planned operation. They deployed their tents in a perfect grid formation, with all the pitches marked out precisely. Each tent was identical in size, colour and shape; each faced in the same direction; and each had a white pennant flying from its peak. When the work was finished the new encampment commanded the whole of the south-east. Along its perimeter ran a low picket fence, and at every corner stood a flagpole.

Isabella, naturally, was outraged.

'What a sight!' she said. 'It's a monstrosity!'

'Well, isn't it just what you envisaged?' I said. 'A vast

sea of tents billowing in the breeze, with flags flying and pennants fluttering aloft?'

'Those tents don't billow,' she retorted. 'They're much too stiff.'

It was the evening of the same day, and we were all gathered beneath Hartopp's awning. Despite his lavish hospitality, the meeting had the sombre undercurrent of a secret conclave. The chief subject of debate was the incursion in the south-east, but Isabella was now voicing wider concerns.

'What the field needs is variety,' she continued. 'We don't want row upon row of identical tents: we want marquees, douars, shāmiyānas, kibitkas, cabanas, tupiks and pandals; we want pavilions with crenellated decorations and swagged contours; and above all we want gorgeous colours: turquoise, vermilion, indigo, magenta and saffron.'

'Sounds more like a fairground,' remarked Brigant. 'What's wrong with green or brown?'

'Far too bland,' said Isabella.

'You forgot to mention bell tents,' I said. 'They're quite nice.'

Isabella was about to reply when she was interrupted by the strident blast of a trumpet.

'That's the third time today,' said Hollis, after it had fallen silent. 'They must be signalling dawn, noon and dusk.'

'Confounded cheek!' snapped Isabella. 'What gives them the right to disturb the peace?'

'Don't know,' I said, 'but we might have to get used to it.'

'We could go and ask them to pipe down a little,' suggested Hartopp. 'The problem is, they seem rather unsociable.'

We all agreed about that.

Since the moment of their arrival, Julian's people had made not the slightest effort to engage with the rest of us. Indeed, they barely acknowledged our existence. It was almost as if they were being deliberately stand-offish, and it soon began to affect how we saw them. Hartopp was a generous and good-natured person, yet even he was reluctant to go and make their acquaintance.

As a matter of fact there'd been no sign of Julian himself so far, but I assumed he planned to return in the near future. His confederates, meanwhile, showed increasing disregard for their neighbours. Over the next few days they established a highly disruptive routine. Each morning at dawn they announced their presence with a loud trumpet blast, followed by a roll-call, an exercise drill and a general inspection, all before breakfast and plainly without a thought for anyone who might happen to be asleep. An afternoon parade was conducted in the same inconsiderate manner: there was absolutely no respite. Our idyll of tranquillity was rapidly fading into a distant memory. The newcomers had set themselves apart, and in consequence an unseen barrier gradually arose between the south-east and the remainder of the field. The possibility of approaching them, if only to try and improve relations, appeared ever more remote.

After a week, however, they sent round a message saying they had a surplus of milk pudding. They said they were willing to share it with the rest of us if we came into their camp at noon.

All they asked was that we brought our own spoons and dishes.

The messenger's name was Eamont. He was of
lowly status and had no influence or authority.
He'd only been appointed messenger recently
on account of his handwriting, which wasn't faultless,
but which was fairly easy to read. The post gave him
certain privileges, and he considered himself lucky, but
he had no influence or authority. None whatsoever. He
told me all this as we stood waiting outside the cookhouse. Actually he'd told me several times before, but
obviously he'd forgotten. I was now on my fourth visit
to the encampment, and I'd turned up early to enquire
if I might have a few words with Aldebaran on a delicate subject. Eamont said he would see what he could
do, but he couldn't promise anything (he had no influence or authority).

'By the way,' he added, 'it's not a cookhouse: it's a
field kitchen.'

'Oh, sorry,' I said. 'I didn't realize.'

'No need to apologize,' he said. 'Just setting you straight, that's all. We're very particular about these details.'

'Right.'

The sharp blast of a trumpet signalled noon. I thanked Eamont, then went inside to collect my daily ration. The cooks greeted me with a nod as I entered, and I found my spoon and dish already set out at my usual table. I was getting quite used to the high standard of service in the field kitchen, but I had a feeling it wouldn't last much longer: the surplus of milk pudding must surely have been reduced by now. Moreover, the cooks were unlikely to repeat their mistake, so today might be my last chance to speak to Aldebaran.

A quarter of an hour passed and he failed to make an appearance. I finished my pudding, then the cooks cleared away my dish and spoon, returning them a few minutes later, sparkling clean. This confirmed that I was definitely on my final visit to the field kitchen. I waited a little longer. Other diners came and went, but Aldebaran was not among them. I'd just begun to give up hope of seeing him when abruptly the flap parted and he came sweeping in. When he saw me sitting at my table he came straight over.

'Everything alright?' he asked. 'Pudding sweet enough?'

'Yes, thank you,' I replied. 'Very nice.'

He gave me a searching look. 'Was there something else?'

'Actually,' I said, 'it's about the trumpet.'

'Oh, yes?'

'There are some people in the field who find it rather loud.'

'Which people?'

'Isabella, for example. One or two others as well, but especially Isabella.'

'The woman with the crimson tent.'

'Yes.'

Throughout the conversation, Aldebaran had been standing over me. Now he sat down in the seat opposite mine. I noticed he was frowning deeply.

'We were wondering,' I said, 'if the trumpet could be somehow muted.'

He considered the request for several moments.

'That would appease her, would it?' he said at last.

'It might help,' I replied.

There was another pause, and I could tell that Aldebaran had something further to ask me.

The question, when it came, was direct. 'I presume she intends to continue swimming in the river?'

'I don't know,' I said. 'What she does is her affair.'

'Yes, I suppose it is,' said Aldebaran. 'All the same, it would help if we knew for certain.'

'Would it?'

'From our point of view it's fairly important.'

'Well, she's swum every day since she's been here,' I said, 'so I can't imagine her changing her ways now.'

'I see.'

We sat in silence for some minutes while Aldebaran pondered whatever was on his mind, then, all of a sudden, his mood brightened.

'Do you think she'd care to come and inspect the camp?' he enquired.

'Again, I don't know,' I said. 'I really can't answer for Isabella.'

'It's all very spick-and-span at present.'

'I don't doubt it, but I'm afraid you'll have to ask her yourself.'

'Very well,' said Aldebaran, evidently resigned to the fact. 'In the meantime, how about you?'

'Inspect the camp?'

'Of course,' he said. 'You're an honoured guest: you've partaken of our milk pudding.'

'Alright,' I replied. 'Thank you.'

'Come on then. We can start now.'

As we rose from our seats, another thought occurred to him.

'By the way,' he said, 'it's not a trumpet: it's a bugle.'

'Oh, sorry,' I said. 'I didn't realize.'

'No need to apologize,' he remarked. 'Just setting you straight, that's all. We're very particular about these details.'

'Right.'

The two of us went outside and the guided tour began. Aldebaran strode briskly around the camp, explaining its various features as I tagged along behind. Obviously I'd seen many of the tents on previous occasions when I passed by, but now I was obliged to examine their every aspect. Their main characteristics were sturdiness and general utility, and they obviously served an important purpose. In appearance, however, they lacked any grace and charm: consequently, I was soon struggling to pay attention. We walked up and down the perfectly straight rows of tents, and it struck me that Hartopp would have found the tour much more interesting than I did. I was certain he'd have been intrigued by the strict geometric forms on display, not to mention the stout fabric employed. Unfortunately, Hartopp persisted in his refusal to enter the sprawling cantonment, despite my reassurances that the newcomers weren't as bad as they'd first seemed. On several occasions I'd urged him to come and try the milk pudding, which I strongly recommended, but it was all in vain. Hartopp simply didn't want to know. During the past few days Brigant and the others had shown similar intransigence, the result being that I was the only person on Aldebaran's conducted tour.

Finally we emerged into the thoroughfare which separated the command tents from their smaller companions, and I remembered the nickname we'd coined on the day the camp was built.

'We call this the "high street",' I said.

'Yes,' replied Aldebaran, 'so do we.'

The inspection ended where it had begun, outside the field kitchen. We halted by the entrance: I'd left my spoon and dish on the table, planning to collect them before I departed. It was now approaching mid-afternoon. All along the 'high street' the pennants were fluttering in the breeze, and for a few moments I paused to admire the spectacle.

'I see you've altered the design,' I said at length.

Aldebaran followed my gaze, but offered no reply.

'When Julian was here they were emblazoned with the letter J,' I added. 'Now they're plain white.'

Still Aldebaran said nothing. Slightly puzzled by his silence, I glanced at him and saw that he was studying the nearest pennant intently, as though he'd only just noticed it. When at last he spoke, his tone was grave.

'Nobody liked Julian,' he said, 'so we got rid of him.'

I was uncertain how to respond to this news. I'd only met Julian once and we hadn't exactly taken to one another, yet he'd appeared to be a very capable individual and the idea that he'd been 'got rid of' was rather unsettling. Privately I wondered if they had the habit of summarily dispensing with people they didn't like, but I decided it would be best not to pursue the matter further. Instead, I merely nodded as if it was an everyday occurrence, before thanking Aldebaran for the guided tour and heading homeward. It was only after I'd trudged across the field to my tent that I realized I'd forgotten my dish and spoon. By this time the entire encampment had started mustering for the afternoon parade, so I decided to postpone collecting them until a later date.

Next morning I listened attentively for the sound of the bugle, hoping it would be muted as I'd requested. It had been a dark night, and when dawn came the sun tried but failed to break through the gathering clouds. I waited for almost half an hour and heard nothing: the sky turned red, yet there was still no bugle call. I concluded, therefore, that my mission had been more successful than I'd dared hope. Aldebaran had evidently heeded my plea and cancelled the bugle altogether.

'Hmm,' I thought to myself. 'Isabella will be delighted.'

A good while later she took her daily swim, and then came ashore to get dried and dressed. After a polite interlude, I expected to see Eamont approach her tent bearing an invitation to visit the camp. To my surprise, though, there was no sign of him, and I soon discovered the reason why. Around noon another train of baggage and supplies arrived at the far side of the river, accompanied by a host of men in buff-coloured tunics. There were also several women. Immediately the whole of the south-east became a hive of activity, with hordes of people coming and going in all directions: no doubt Eamont was too busy to run up and down with invitations for Isabella. Amongst the supplies I spotted a bulky item which had to be carried across the river by four men. I was unable to tell what it was because it was wrapped in a tarpaulin, and anyway the porters were quickly lost from view amid the milling throng.

The majority of the baggage consisted of tents. These

were swiftly laid out and erected under the watchful eyes of a surveyor, a quartermaster and a clerk of works. I'd often noticed this trio of officials during my visits to the encampment, and I presumed they acted as deputies to Aldebaran. From what I observed, they were always highly efficient. Before the end of the day, a new row of tents was established and the camp's perimeter extended.

In the early evening I went over to see Hen. He was the person least affected by the developments in the south-east, and I looked forward to a refreshing conversation with someone who didn't constantly complain about the newcomers. On this point my wishes were met: Hen was apparently unconcerned about the enlargement of the camp. I was taken aback, however, by his response when I told him what had happened to Julian. I recounted what Aldebaran had said, and when I finished Hen raised his eyebrows.

'I would have thought,' he remarked, 'that you'd be more worried about Thomas than Julian.'

'Oh, yes, Thomas,' I said. 'I'd forgotten all about him.'

'Forgotten?' said Hen, plainly astonished. 'But he's one of us.'

'Oh, I'm not sure about that,' I said.

'Of course he is,' Hen declared. 'He was amongst the first here.'

I peered at Hen with mild disbelief. It struck me that he was being surprisingly loyal to Thomas, considering the rival claims of days gone by. Clearly his perceptions had altered. At the same moment I realized that my own loyalty was to the Great Field itself, rather than any particular person (and especially not Thomas). Nonetheless, I had no desire to fall out with Hen, so I simply shrugged and remained silent.

'For all we know, Thomas could be in all sorts of difficulty,' Hen continued. 'He left with Julian's people, seemingly of his own accord, but it's obvious there's been a change of circumstance.'

'Yes,' I conceded, 'I suppose so.'

'Perhaps you could find out more.'

'Me?' I said. 'How can I find out?'

'You're friendly with them, aren't you?' replied Hen. 'You know who's in charge over there.'

'Yes, it's Aldebaran,' I said, 'but he never really tells me anything. Most of the time he's busy asking questions about Isabella.'

'And you answer them?'

'Yes, usually.'

'Singing for your supper,' said Hen.

'No, you're wrong,' I said. 'I accept their hospitality, that's all: I'm very partial to their milk pudding.'

Hen shook his head solemnly.

'Well,' he said, 'we'll see.'

I returned to my tent feeling slightly disquieted by Hen's comments. It had begun to dawn on me that I may have incurred a cost for all those liberal helpings I'd enjoyed. I should have known better. It was one thing being an 'honoured guest' in the encampment: it was quite another to be derided by my companions. I resolved to be careful in future about where I went and what I said to whom.

As it happened, the newcomers focused more attention on Isabella than all the rest of us put together. After a few days she received a visit from Eamont. I witnessed the event at a distance but, even so, I could see he was looking rather harassed. He brought a note informing Isabella that a command tent had been set aside for her exclusive use. Within its walls were a copper bath and an ample supply of hot water. A selection of soaps and freshly laundered towels had been provided, and a number of handmaidens would be in attendance at all hours. Could she please be so kind as to accept the offer forthwith?

Needless to say, Eamont returned to the camp thoroughly disappointed. His superiors had clearly gone to the utmost lengths to win Isabella over, yet despite their blandishments she maintained her custom of bathing naked in the river. I could have told them they were wasting their efforts from the very start, but they never asked me.

In the meantime, the weather continued to deteriorate. Across the entire field, all the flags and pennants were at full stretch. There was definitely some rain on the way. Over in the north-east, Hartopp began to prepare for the oncoming deluge, cautiously adjusting his awnings and tightening his guy ropes. Likewise, Brigant improved his defences with an oilcloth flysheet.

By now, of course, we'd all heard about Isabella rejecting the invitation. Brigant and I discussed it one afternoon as the sky darkened.

'It sounded most luxurious,' I said. 'Hot water in abundance, handmaidens, freshly laundered towels.'

'Decadent, more like,' uttered Brigant.

'To tell the truth, I would welcome a hot bath myself.'

'Maybe so,' he said, 'but it's Isabella they're trying to tame, not you.'

'I'm fully aware of that,' I replied. 'Still, it's a pity the bath's gone unused, especially with the weather on the turn.'

'Why?' said Brigant. 'Are you finding life in the field too tough?'

'No.'

'Well stop being so soft then!'

This wasn't the first time Brigant had spoken in such terms. He was becoming increasingly intolerant of the soft life, as he called it. Other targets included frailty and decadence, but the general heading was softness (he tended to forget that he was once quite soft himself). It all arose from his division of the field into upper and lower parts. The division was purely notional, a product of his own invention, but Brigant was unbending in his belief. Over recent weeks he'd developed the idea further, and concluded that life became steadily harder the higher up the slope someone lived, as if it was a sort of sliding scale. Personally, I couldn't see any difference: we all endured exactly the same weather conditions, seasonal changes and so on. Moreover, as I mentioned before, the slope barely amounted to anything; indeed it was scarcely perceptible, a minor inconvenience at worst. Nevertheless, Brigant insisted that life was harsher in the upper field.

His theory was about to be put to the test. After another day of threatening skies and rising winds, the rain finally came sweeping in. It was heavy and unremitting and didn't cease for a week, during which period we were all confined to our tents. In these circumstances, there was nothing to do except wait patiently for the end. Even so, we had to endure a very dreary spell. For hour after hour, I listened to the sound of rain drumming on my roof. When I peeked out through my opening I could see the entire south-eastern encampment reduced to an indeterminate blur of dripping canvas; there was no sign of movement; puddles were forming in the avenues; and even the numerous flags and pennants were hanging down limp and wet. Over in the north-east, Hartopp's angular tent appeared equally lifeless, though no doubt he was sheltering under his awning, eagerly testing its resistance to the weather and recording the facts for future reference. Meanwhile, hunched beneath his flysheet, Brigant sat and glowered at the driving rain.

Eventually my gaze fell on Isabella's tent, faraway to the east. I'd never been invited beyond its tasselled portal, but I assumed the interior was dry, warm and cosy. I knew it was furnished with a tapestry and a collection of velvet cushions: I'd watched her carefully installing them on the day she arrived. There was also an eiderdown. Apart from that I knew nothing. She'd positioned her tent facing west so that she could catch the sun going down at the end of each day. As a consequence, it lay in my direct line of vision. I'd seen it on countless occasions and could even picture it with my eyes closed. Isabella's door was always in view, yet she remained forever unapproachable. She'd made it plain from the beginning that she preferred to be alone; she was independent and forthright; furthermore, as her admirers had discovered, she was notoriously difficult to please. Still, I continued to live in hope. Isabella's tent was crimson on the outside, sometimes flaring into fiery red, but I liked to imagine it was lined with cloth of gold.

When at last the rain subsided, I emerged to find the ground underfoot very wet indeed. It made coming and going unpleasant for a day or two. The problem was most pronounced in the south-east. No sooner had the sky cleared than I saw Aldebaran and his officials pacing around the encampment, prodding at the turf with rods and generally assessing the situation. Later I saw several of their men digging gullies between the tents. Obviously the area was waterlogged and they were taking appropriate measures.

Ever since arriving, the newcomers had seldom ventured

beyond their self-imposed boundary: this was a point which had always stood in their favour. For some reason they were only interested in occupying their own corner, and the rest of the field they left untouched. I was intrigued, therefore, when I noticed the surveyor and an assistant walking along the river bank in the east. The assistant was carrying a large spool of string, a mallet and some wooden pegs. I saw Isabella peering out at them as they skirted her crimson tent, but they continued on their way with no more than a polite nod. I could now see that the surveyor was taking very deliberate strides, as if gauging a particular distance. Finally, the two of them came to a halt. The assistant knocked a peg into the ground and attached the string. Next, the surveyor produced an object from his pocket and examined it closely. It transpired that this was a compass; in due course he despatched his assistant westward with the spool of string, the mallet and another peg. The string was gradually paid out as he advanced across the field. I thought he passed unnecessarily close to Brigant's tent (there was, after all, plenty of room on either side), but he pressed on regardless. Fortunately, Brigant was elsewhere at the time. When the string ran out the assistant stopped and waited. He hadn't quite reached Hen's territory in the extreme west, but apparently he'd gone far enough to satisfy the surveyor. At a given signal he knocked the second peg into the ground and pulled the string tight. Immediately it snagged on Brigant's tent. The surveyor gave it a flick from his end to try and straighten it, but again it snagged. Unperturbed, the assistant tied the string to the peg and returned to join the surveyor. After a brief discussion, they headed back along the river towards the camp.

As soon as they were out of sight, I went over to investigate. The string was fairly taut and chafed against Brigant's flysheet. Patently the plan had been to set out a straight line between the pegs, but the tent had got in the way.

'What's going on here?' said a voice beside me. It belonged to Brigant. He'd been visiting Hartopp and had just come back. I explained to him about the surveyor and his assistant.

'Well,' he said, 'couldn't they have asked me before they started?'

'You weren't here,' I replied. 'Maybe they decided to leave it till tomorrow and then ask.'

'Yes, maybe,' said Brigant, although he didn't sound convinced.

We were still debating the matter when Isabella arrived. She'd observed the episode with the string and was naturally incensed.

'You should march into their camp,' she told Brigant, 'and demand they remove that string at once!'

'I can't be bothered,' he said. 'It's probably easier to shift my tent.'

'You can't do that!' said Isabella. 'You'd be giving in to them.'

'Really, I don't mind,' said Brigant, with a sigh. 'All I want is a quiet life. Besides, I've been thinking of moving further up the field for a good while now. It's more interesting in the north.'

Despite Isabella's protestations, Brigant was adamant, so later the same day I went and helped him take his tent down. He chose a pitch some distance up the slope, and together we moved everything.

'It'll be good to get that trumpet out of earshot,' he remarked, when we'd finished our work.

I was tempted to correct Brigant on two counts, but I thought better of it and made no comment.

The offending length of string now lay perfectly straight across the field. Next morning, the surveyor and his assistant returned for a brief inspection, nodded their heads in approval, then went away again.

Around noon, when milk pudding was normally being served in the field kitchen, a small party of men left the encampment and followed the river to the spot where the string line began. They were carrying spades, pick-axes and shovels. It was a slightly odd scene: despite their plentiful stock of tools, these characters seemed distinctly unworkmanlike. They straggled along dragging their heels, and were plainly in no hurry to begin whatever task they'd been assigned. In this respect they were quite different from the other men in the camp: the majority performed their duties with flawless efficiency. The present bunch, by contrast, hardly knew where to start.

They stood around, gawping at the peg and the length of string as though they'd never seen such items before; then they turned and gazed haplessly into the west. Eventually one of them started poking at the ground with his spade, but to such little effect that he soon gave up. Another tried a pick-axe, and similarly failed to make any impression. I was getting frustrated just watching their antics, so after a while I strolled casually across the field, drifting in their general direction but trying my best to remain aloof. I didn't really want to get involved with the newcomers again, but on the other hand I was interested to know what they were trying to do. There was no harm, I reasoned, in taking a closer look.

I received a shock, however, as I drew nearer the gang of workers. All at once I recognized the cooks from the field kitchen: the very same men who until recently had stirred my milk pudding. Among them was the cook who'd served me on my first visit to the encampment. His name was Yadegarian and he'd told me about the various types of pudding on offer. As I recalled, his advice had been most helpful. I'd met his colleagues on subsequent days, and they'd struck me as a friendly bunch. Today, though, I couldn't help noticing how downcast they all appeared. When they saw me approaching they ceased their futile endeavours and regarded me listlessly.

'Hello,' I said. 'What are you fellows doing here?'

'We're supposed to be digging a trench,' said Yadegarian, 'but we're not really cut out for this sort of work.'

'So why've you got to do it?'

By way of answer, he and the other cooks merely bowed their heads. It was almost as if they were ashamed of something.

'Are you in trouble?' I asked.

They all looked at one another for a moment, then Yadegarian spoke.

'Yes,' he said, 'we are.'

'Why?'

'We produced a shortage of milk pudding. We measured the ingredients in the wrong quantities.'

'Not again!'

'I'm afraid so.'

'And this is your punishment?'

'Yes.'

'Good grief,' I said. 'What kind of regime is it, exactly?'

The cooks ventured no opinion. Instead, they just stood there, silent and forlorn.

I puffed out my cheeks and stared thoughtfully at the length of string stretching away into the distance.

'Well,' I said, 'it looks as if you've no choice but to get on with the job.'

'But we've no idea how to do it!' protested Yadegarian. He was plainly very concerned.

'Don't worry about that,' I replied. 'I can give you a few pointers.'

'Such as?'

'Well, for instance, you're all wearing sandals. They're

wholly inappropriate for heavy labouring: you'd be much better off in proper workboots.'

I indicated my own footwear.

'Ah, yes,' said Yadegarian, with a glimmer of recognition. 'I think we can get those from our quartermaster.'

'Good,' I said. 'As soon as possible then.'

'Alright.'

With a wave of my hand I grouped the cooks around me so they could see what I was talking about.

'Next,' I continued, 'you'll need to learn about the wide range of tools at your disposal. Each has a specific role: pick-axes are for breaking up the earth; spades are for digging; shovels are for excavation: you'll soon get the hang of it and then I can show you how to use them correctly.'

In order to get the job started, I grabbed a spade and dug the first section of ground myself. The going was fairly easy, and I soon had the beginnings of a trench. Alongside it lay a neat pile of earth.

'There you are,' I said. 'Just use the string line as a guide and it should be nice and straight when it's finished.'

Obviously I couldn't leave them unsupervised, at least not until they'd tried doing it themselves, so I watched while they took turns with the spades, shovels and picks. Initially they struggled, but I offered plenty of encouragement and gradually they developed a suitable work rate. Even so, it had become clear that digging the trench was no small undertaking. By my reckoning, the job could last four or five days. In the meantime, I assumed the cooks were excused kitchen duties. When I asked them, however, they all shook their heads.

'The demands of the kitchen remain the same,' explained Yadegarian. 'We're having to get up extra early just to keep on top of everything.'

'How early?'

'Well, this morning we were baking biscuits before dawn.'

'Really?' I said. 'I like biscuits.'

'They're our speciality,' said Yadegarian.

'Not milk pudding?'

'No.'

I mentioned that Hartopp was a keen advocate of biscuits and always maintained a copious stock; but Yadegarian seemed too preoccupied by the present task to absorb the information. It was patently weighing heavily upon him.

Naturally, I felt rather guilty about standing idly by when the cooks had been working all hours. Therefore, I decided to pitch in and help them finish the trench. I selected a shovel as my weapon of choice; then I set to and laboured until late afternoon. With an extra man in the team we made excellent progress, though the cooks began to flag when evening drew near. Finally, at dusk, I suggested we called a halt, and they thanked me for my assistance before wandering back to the encampment. The trench was starting to take definite shape and form, and as I gazed at our handiwork I suddenly realized that neither Hartopp, Brigant nor any of the others had been over to have a look. It was too late now, of course, because it was almost dark, but I was surprised that nobody had come and shown any interest in the project. Actually, when I thought about it, they were all notice-able by their absence, and vaguely I wondered what could be the reason.

On the third evening I received a visit from Aldebaran. I was tidying up after another day's work when I saw him approaching from the south-east, evidently with the purpose of inspecting the trench. I was glad to see him: the job was three-quarters complete and I was looking forward to showing him what we'd accomplished. Our trench was deep and wide and unerringly straight, all in accordance with the surveyor's plans. As a matter of fact, I was so pleased with the cooks that I'd let them go off slightly earlier than usual. I thought they'd earned a bit of a break, especially since it had been so warm during the afternoon. The fine weather had returned at last, and in the dry conditions we'd made good headway. Now, with night falling, the sky was tinged pink and silver. As the sun sank towards the horizon, Aldebaran's advancing figure cast a long shadow across the field.

When he reached the trench he paused and stood peering in.

'Exemplary,' he declared. 'Should be very effective.'

'Couple more days and it'll be finished,' I said, 'providing the weather holds.'

'I gather you've taken charge of the operation.'

'Yes, I have,' I affirmed. 'They seem to work much better when they receive direct orders.'

'Indeed.' Aldebaran reflected for a moment, and then said, 'It's a shame we can't reward you with some milk pudding. Unfortunately, there's been a hiatus in the production process and we've run out entirely.'

'I know,' I said. 'The cooks told me all about it.'

Aldebaran glanced at me.

'Been blubbing to you, have they?' he asked.

'No, on the contrary,' I replied, 'they've taken their punishment in their stride.'

'Really?'

'They're turning into a proper workforce.'

'Then plainly we're in your debt.'

'Think nothing of it,' I said. 'Glad to be of assistance.'

After this courteous exchange I accompanied Aldebaran as he walked the length of the trench. For a while he was silent, but then another thought occurred to him.

'By the way,' he said, 'it's not punishment: it's discipline.'

'Oh, sorry,' I said. 'I didn't realize.'

'No need to apologize,' he remarked. 'Just setting you straight, that's all. We're very particular about these details.'

'Right.'

The inspection now being over, Aldebaran murmured some pleasantry and departed. I spent a few minutes watching the sunset, then returned to the comparative comfort of my tent. I slept well that night, just as I had every night since I'd been involved with the venture. It had been hard graft, but quite fulfilling in its own way, and now the end was in sight.

During the course of the excavations, an earthwork had been raised along one side of the trench. We'd made a fairly good job of it, packing the earth hard so that it wouldn't collapse, then crowning it with a layer of turf. The resulting embankment looked formidable, a landmark in its own right, but it was soon to be a source of dissension.

Around mid-afternoon on the fourth day I was toiling alone in the middle section of the trench, making sure that it ran evenly. For various reasons I'd become separated from my co-workers who were further over to the west, but I could still hear occasional snatches of distant conversation. I stopped and listened. Several times in recent days I'd tried to explain to them that talking on the job was a distraction which reduced productivity. Nevertheless, they persisted in chattering whenever my back was turned. I was just about to walk along the trench and reprimand them, when a familiar voice addressed me from directly above. I looked up and saw Brigant standing on the edge, gazing down.

'I suppose they're satisfied now, are they?' he said.

'Who?' I enquired.

'Those people from the camp.'

'Oh, well,' I said, 'yes, they do seem rather pleased with the outcome.'

'I'm sure they do,' said Brigant. 'In fact, they must be delighted. They made it clear from the beginning they wanted to exclude us, and now they've built a wall to prove it.'

I leaned on my shovel and stared at him with disbelief.

'Where'd you get that idea?' I said. 'Of course it's not a wall.'

'What is it then?' asked Brigant.

'It's for drainage.'

At this moment, a second face loomed into view. It belonged to Hartopp.

'Looks like a wall to me,' he said.

'I'd go further than that,' proclaimed Brigant. 'I'd describe it as nothing less than a defensive rampart.'

'Nonsense,' I said. 'It's for drainage, pure and simple. You know how wet the ground gets in the south-east. That last dose of rainfall was the worst in months. It almost flooded their tents, so they decided to find a remedy.'

'But we get more rain in the upper field,' said Brigant.

'Possibly,' I replied, 'but it all drains into the south-east: that's why the grass is so rich and lush.'

Hartopp peered into the trench.

'It's completely dry,' he said. 'Who told you it was for drainage?'

'Nobody, really,' I said, 'but it's obvious it must be.'

'It's just as obvious it's a wall,' remarked Brigant. 'A wall of earth.'

Just then, Yadegarian came walking along the trench. When he saw the three of us talking he stopped in his tracks.

'Everything alright here?' he asked, eyeing Hartopp and Brigant intently.

All at once I realized he'd never met them before; nor they him.

'Yes, everything's fine,' I said quickly. 'Yadegarian, may I introduce Hartopp and Brigant? Brigant, Hartopp: this is Yadegarian.'

There followed a polite yet awkward exchange of greetings, after which Hartopp and Brigant retired a short distance.

'I've just come to tell you,' said Yadegarian, 'that we've reached the end of the string line.'

'Ah, good,' I answered. 'No more digging then?'

'Just tidying up,' he said, 'and then we'll be finished.'

'Alright, I'll be along to have a look in a minute.'

After Yadegarian had gone, I scrambled out of the trench and joined Hartopp and Brigant. They were scrutinizing the embankment with undisguised mistrust, and to some extent I could understand why they felt aggrieved: from where they stood it indeed had the semblance of an imposing wall. At the same time, however, I thought they were both being a little unreasonable. The raised earthwork was an inevitable consequence of the drainage scheme and couldn't be helped: surely they could see that? As for Brigant's assertion that it rained more in the upper field, well, frankly, I'd never heard anything so preposterous. Rain was rain as far as I was concerned, and had the same effect everywhere, but Brigant saw it all differently. He seemed to think that hardship and discomfort were the sole preserve of the north; and that such conditions were unheard of in the south, east or west; he was becoming increasingly outspoken on the subject and now, apparently, he'd infected Hartopp with a similar malaise; hence, their concerted criticism of the so-called 'wall'. Moreover, Brigant gave the impression that he'd been forcibly displaced by the construction work, whereas in truth he'd opted to move northward of his own volition. He evidently regarded the embankment as a kind of personal affront, and I realized I was incapable of changing his outlook.

Before we parted he delivered a final broadside. 'You're fortunate you didn't try to build it any further north,' he said. 'Otherwise you'd have run into flinty ground: that would have put a stop to your game.'

'How do you know what's in the ground?' I asked. 'I've never seen you digging.'

'Believe me,' said Brigant. 'I just know.'

Hartopp's standpoint was equally uncompromising. I'd expected him to view the earthwork through the eyes of an engineer: after all, it was quite an achievement and made a majestic sight as it traversed the Great Field from east to west. In addition, it was perfectly straight, which I hoped would appeal to his geometric inclinations. Instead, though, he judged it to be a gross infringement. In this sense, he shared Brigant's perspective: as they saw it, they were forever being imposed upon by outsiders, offcomers and interlopers; and the earthwork was merely the most recent example.

Feeling rather disappointed, I left the pair of them nursing their grievances and went back to join my workmates. I'd neglected Yadegarian and the others slightly longer than intended, so I was pleased to find them putting the finishing touches to the job. Standing nearby was Hen. He, too, had been wary of the trench when the work began: he'd assumed the excavations were heading directly into his camp, but once I'd convinced him otherwise he'd observed our progress with friendly detachment. Also, he'd discovered that the cooks shared his affinity with the west: seemingly, there was a certain quality in the daylight which reminded them of their distant homeland. They even talked of settling in the west, if only their employers would allow it. Sadly, this was out of the question.

'We have to do as we're told,' said Yadegarian. 'Tomorrow we'll be baking biscuits again.'

Hen mentioned to me privately that he wasn't sure whether he liked the people in charge of the encampment. In his opinion the cooks were being severely overworked for little or no recompense. Furthermore, there had been absolutely no public consultation when the trench was commissioned: the project had simply started without any warning. True enough, he said, they'd made no attempt as yet to encroach on his part of the field; but who could tell where their future ambitions may lie?

'It was much better when Thomas held the south-east,' Hen concluded. 'He always treated boundaries with respect.'

After the cooks had tidied up, I asked them to collect together all the entrenching tools so they could be returned to the quartermaster. This was a minor chore, likely to take a few minutes at the most. While I waited, I pondered Hen's words and decided he had scant cause for alarm.

There was, of course, one other person who hadn't been consulted. Isabella's tent was situated in the east of the field, which meant she stood to gain from the improvements. Even so, she'd shown a conspicuous lack of interest in the ongoing work, preferring to spend her time bathing undisturbed in the river. This was wholly understandable: the drainage scheme was hardly glamorous and, besides, the commencement of the trench had coincided with the return of the warm weather. Isabella remained gloriously disengaged, far from the hustle and bustle, and we hadn't seen much of her for days. Therefore, I was caught unawares when she suddenly appeared at the foot of the embankment.

She was looking as radiant as ever.

'Finished all your digging, have you?' she asked.

'Yes,' I replied. 'The job's complete.'

'That's good,' she said. 'So, when are you planning to fill it back in?'

'We're not.'

'I beg your pardon?'

'We're not filling it back in.'

'What!' Isabella's face darkened. 'You can't leave it like this!'

'It's perfectly normal practice,' I said. 'An open trench is most effective.'

'But you've ruined our beautiful meadow!'

'Well, not me personally.'

'Yes, you personally!' she snapped. 'You can't blame anyone else!'

'But I was only helping.'

'No, you weren't! You practically took the job over! It's been the same from the very start: you just can't resist sticking your nose in! Ever since those people arrived, you've gone out of your way to do their dirty work, no matter how much disruption you cause, no matter how much irretrievable loss; and you do it all for a mess of pottage!'

Isabella fell silent and stood glaring at me with unconcealed resentment.

'Milk pudding, actually,' I said.

The remark was intended to lighten the tone of the conversation, but I knew at once that it was a mistake.

'Cross me at your peril,' said Isabella, before turning and marching away.

I watched her diminishing figure as she headed across the field; and I wondered how on earth I could ever regain her favour. Even worse, I realized that the entire tirade had been witnessed by the cooks. They'd finished collecting the tools and were now waiting quietly nearby.

'My apologies for that,' I said. 'She's not very happy about the trench.'

'No,' replied Yadegarian, 'so we gathered.'

'Got everything then?'

'Not quite,' he said. 'A couple of the spades are missing.'

'Ah.'

'We've searched all over the place but there's no sign of them.'

'Perhaps they'll turn up in a day or two.'

'Yes, perhaps.'

'I'll keep a sharp lookout.'

'Thanks.'

The moment had come to disband our fledgling

workforce. I shook hands with each of them; then they set off towards the encampment.

'I'll see you when I drop in for my dish and spoon,' I said.

'Alright,' said Yadegarian. 'Bye.'

When I returned to my tent I discovered it had gone slack in my absence. It was in a very sorry state: plainly I'd been so concerned with the trench that I'd failed to carry out any basic maintenance. The fault was easily rectified, a question of tightening a few guy ropes, but it did nothing to reduce the sense of gloom that threatened to engulf me. The job's termination had left me with a profound feeling of emptiness. Not only had I parted with the cooks who I'd been working alongside all week, but I was now in danger of being ostracized by my friends and neighbours. Indeed, judging by recent events, I was close to becoming an outcast.

A few days later, however, I was given the chance to redeem my reputation. Around dusk I received a visit from Hartopp's younger son Eldred. Like his father, he was an amiable person and I was pleasantly surprised when he turned up at my doorway. Nonetheless, he'd chosen an unusual time to come calling. It was almost dark when he arrived, and I also noticed that he approached by a circuitous route, rather than crossing the field directly. All this suggested some kind of subterfuge was afoot, and when he spoke in hushed tones my suspicions were confirmed.

'Isabella's looking for volunteers,' he said quietly. 'She intends to harry the south-east.'

'Is this because of the trench?' I enquired.

'Yes, partly,' said Eldred, 'but we're fed up with the newcomers in general, so we want to teach them a lesson.'

'Who's we?'

'So far it's Isabella, Hollis and me, but you're more than welcome to join us.'

'And what's the plan?'

'We're going to raid the encampment and let down a few of their tents.'

He was unable to provide further details, and I began to wonder if any of this had been properly thought through. It didn't seem to have occurred to Eldred (or, more likely, Isabella) that what they proposed was the equivalent of pulling a tiger's tail. Letting down other people's tents was undoubtedly satisfying, but it was bound to lead to reprisals. Moreover, it would be quite obvious who the culprits were. The notion of 'harrying the south-east' may have sounded romantic to these youngsters, but it was a sure-fire recipe for trouble.

Even if these qualms had been set aside, though, I would still have felt reluctant to get involved with the conspiracy. From a personal viewpoint I'd always found the newcomers both courteous and civil, despite their random displays of insensitivity. The fact that I'd partaken of their milk pudding also needed to be considered. I had no wish to be seen as their lackey (which Isabella had so forcefully implied), but at the same time I harboured no particular gripe against them. On balance, then, I decided not to participate in the raid.

I explained my reasons to Eldred, and he accepted them with good grace before bidding me farewell and heading back to the north-east. All the same, he was certain to report our exchange to Isabella: consequently, I'd be even deeper in her bad books. Still, I wasn't prepared to change my mind.

After Eldred had gone, it struck me that the plotters had overlooked a far easier target. The south-eastern enclave was densely populated, whereas the trench lay unmanned and ripe for sabotage. Equipped with the correct tools, a dedicated team could inflict a lot of damage in a few hours, destroying what the cooks and I had taken days to create. It was a definite possibility, and when I remembered the missing spades I realized it could be happening at this very moment! Quickly I went out to investigate, padding noiselessly across the field in starlight until I arrived at the looming embankment. Fortunately, the trench appeared to have escaped the attention of Isabella and her accomplices: there was nobody else around.

I stopped and peered into the brooding silence of the north. A desultory breeze was blowing, and I could see the distant flicker of lights inside the scattered tents. Eldred had failed to inform me whether Hartopp or Brigant were privy to the planned raid, but anyway I felt unable to discuss the subject with either of them. Hen, meanwhile, was an unknown quantity. All I knew for sure was that the trench was vulnerable to attack, and as the evening passed I began to consider what safeguards could be put in place. Needless to say, these were few and far between. By the following morning I'd reached the conclusion that my only option was to mount irregular patrols along the trench (regular patrols would plainly attract interest and risked putting ideas into people's heads).

So it was that I became a sort of unsung vigilante.

My first few forays were relatively easy: I simply waited until everyone was up and about, then I wandered slowly back and forth, pretending to search for the missing spades. At one point I met Brigant coming the other way, and asked him if he happened to have seen them during his travels. He said he hadn't, but he promised to keep a lookout.

Later patrols required more circumspection. Clearly I couldn't go over the same ground again and again, so in due course I discontinued the 'search' and reverted to taking casual strolls across the field. I soon learned that the trick was to affect an air of nonchalance and never look directly at anyone or anything in particular. Occasionally I drifted up to the very north, so that I could get an overall picture of developments as they unfolded. In truth, though, there was very little happening that could be counted as suspicious activity: despite simmering animosity towards the south-east, the field remained as quiet as ever.

On the other hand, it was inconceivable that Isabella would abandon her plans. Therefore, I knew it was only a question of time before she and her northern allies made their move.

This, when it finally came, was rather predictable. In the small hours of the next moonless night I was woken by a series of wild whoopings, followed by the martial tones of a bugle. Within minutes the whole encampment was in uproar. Apparently the raid was a success, but when daylight came there was precious little to show for it: a handful of buff-coloured tents lay collapsed or at crazy angles from having their guy ropes unfastened. That was all that had been achieved. The occupants soon got them straightened out; then they turned and gazed bemusedly at their distant neighbours. Shortly afterwards, Aldebaran appeared on the scene.

Retribution was equally swift. Later the same morning, while Isabella was bathing in the river, half a dozen men emerged from the encampment and headed for her crimson tent. I watched aghast as they set to work, flattening it completely and pulling out all the pegs. They actually showed considerable restraint (they could have done far worse); nevertheless, when Isabella returned she was furious. Also, she was quick to note that none of the other settlers had received similar treatment: she alone had been punished for the night's exploits. Naturally, we all rushed over to help her get sorted out, but she was unforgiving.

'Why didn't anybody try and stop them?' she demanded.

'We were having breakfast,' said Hartopp. 'We didn't notice.'

'I was asleep,' said Brigant.

'I was looking west,' said Hen.

'Really?' murmured Isabella. 'How convenient.' Lastly she turned to me. 'And what's your excuse?'

'I haven't got one,' I said. 'Sorry.'

She gave me a long, meaningful stare before dismissing each and every one of us.

'Off you go,' she said. 'I can fix all this on my own.'

'Well, if you need any assistance,' said Hartopp, 'just let us know.'

Isabella made no response, and we all traipsed away in shamefaced silence.

The next day she arose early and went down to the south-west corner of the field, where she spent several hours cutting reeds and laying them in the sun to dry. I had an odd feeling about this, so eventually I walked across to say hello. Isabella saw me coming, but she ignored my approach and continued with her task.

'I see you've been busy,' I ventured.

'Yes,' she replied, avoiding my gaze.

I glanced at the lengths of cut reed which lay all around. 'Not building a boat, are you?'

'Yes, actually, I am,' she said. 'I'm leaving.'

'But you can't leave,' I said. 'The place wouldn't be the same without you.'

'Can't be helped,' said Isabella. 'I've decided to follow the sun.'

She ceased her labours and stood back to survey the situation. She'd accomplished a great deal in those few hours, and there were plenty enough reeds to make a boat.

'I hope you're not going because of me,' I said.

'Don't flatter yourself!' snapped Isabella, finally turning in my direction. 'I was going anyway!'

'Why?'

'Because the field's been spoilt,' she said. 'It's lost its innocence.'

As if to underline her pronouncement, the blast of a bugle signalled noon. Previous orders, it seemed, had been revoked.

Isabella peered towards the south-east.

'Bunch of ruffians,' she remarked.

'Not entirely,' I said. 'In some respects they're quite a civilizing influence.'

'Oh yes?'

'Marvellous organizational skills; iron discipline; proper plans and surveys; spacious thoroughfares; sophisticated drainage systems; monumental earthworks; communal kitchens and bakeries; bathhouses with hot water freely available. The list goes on and on.'

'Well,' said Isabella, 'they may think they're civilized, but they're certainly not gentlemen.'

Over subsequent days, various attempts were made to

113

dissuade Isabella from leaving. She was visited in turn by Brigant, Hen and Hartopp (accompanied by his two contrite sons), and showered with compliments and bouquets. They promised they'd do anything she asked, if only she would stay. It was all to no avail, of course: Isabella wasn't listening any more. Instead, she continued with her work. Once the reeds were sufficiently dry, she twisted them together into a strong, pliable fibre which she carried in bundles to the east; then she began skilfully fashioning a boat. We looked on with admiration as it gradually took form. Hartopp, Hollis and Eldred were especially fascinated, having never seen Isabella's original vessel, but they felt obliged to keep their distance and could only observe from afar. Finally, when it was complete, she hauled it to the water's edge. It was sleek and elegant, with a high, curved prow.

The following morning, I watched from my doorway as Isabella made ready to leave. Without ceremony, she took down her crimson tent, folded it, and stowed it in the boat. Her other possessions were stacked nearby, ready for loading, and all at once she turned and beckoned me to join her. Quickly, and with renewed hope, I crossed the field to where she stood waiting.

'Right, I'm off now,' she said in a businesslike manner. 'You'd better give these back to your friends.'

Isabella reached amongst the assorted baggage and produced two shiny spades.

'Oh,' I said, 'we wondered where they'd got to.'

'Yes, well, I thought I might need them,' she said, 'but I don't now.'

By this time, Hartopp and the others had arrived to witness Isabella's departure. When she saw them she bristled with irritation.

'I don't want any fuss,' she announced. 'Keep out of the way please.'

She pushed her boat into the shallows, loaded the last few items, then stepped aboard. A minute later she was in the middle of the river, floating steadily downstream.

'Bye, Isabella!' we all chorused, and she raised her arm in salute.

As she disappeared around the furthest curve, I noticed a flock of excited birds whirling overhead.

I suspected that Yadegarian and his colleagues would be in trouble for losing the spades, so it was imperative to get them returned as quickly as possible. For a while I considered smuggling them into the encampment when I went to collect my dish and spoon, but in reality I knew this was unfeasible: they were far too large to conceal in my clothing. Ultimately, therefore, I decided that openness was the best policy. I waited for the quiet period between breakfast and dinner; then I grabbed the spades and set off towards the field kitchen.

It soon became clear that I needn't have worried: there were plainly more important matters at hand than a couple of missing spades. The moment I entered the camp I sensed it was in a state of disarray. The change was only slight, hardly anything really, but even so the signs were unmistakable: the flags and pennants looked ragged and worn, the avenues were deeply rutted, and some of the tents had begun to fade in the sunlight. I was contemplating all this when Aldebaran emerged from a side alley. He seemed rather distracted and almost walked straight past me.

'Hello, Aldebaran,' I said.

He stopped and peered in my direction.

'Sorry,' he said, 'I was miles away.'

'I'm just bringing these spades back.'

'Ah, good.'

'Isabella borrowed them for a day or two.'

'Isabella,' he intoned. 'She's gone now, hasn't she?'

'Yes,' I replied, 'she left this morning.'

Aldebaran nodded his approval.

'We didn't mean to drive her away,' he said, 'but frankly we found her very difficult.'

'Yes, so I surmised.'

'We bent over backwards to accommodate her, yet all she did was bombard us with complaints and criticism.'

'Well,' I said, 'I'm going to miss her all the same.'

Aldebaran gave no answer, and when I glanced at him I realized I'd lost his attention. Obviously his mind was focused on other concerns, so I made my excuses and slipped away.

When I entered the field kitchen, I discovered further evidence of decline: the great cast-iron cooking pots were still ranged along the counter, but now they all stood cold and unused. Yadegarian was working nearby, cutting a loaf of bread into very thin slices. We exchanged greetings, then I handed him the two spades.

'I'd forgotten all about these,' he remarked. 'Thanks, though. I'll put them in the store when the quartermaster's not looking.'

'You weren't in trouble then?'

'No,' said Yadegarian. 'Actually he didn't even notice they were missing, he's been so busy.'

'What with?'

'Logistical problems mainly. For some reason the supply lines have failed and our provisions are running low.'

'Oh dear.'

'We've enough to feed the few, but not the many, so we'll soon be going onto half rations.'

'Any idea what's caused it?'

'None at all. Eamont set off a couple of days ago to see if he could find out, but so far there's been no word from him.'

Apparently the cooks had received instructions that all bread was to be toasted so it would last longer. Yadegarian loaded the grill and asked me to keep an eye on it while he sought out my dish and spoon.

'They're perfectly safe,' he assured me, 'but I can't quite remember where we put them. Probably out the back somewhere. Won't be a minute.'

With that, he vanished into a recess at the rear of the kitchen. I heard him rummaging through various crates and boxes, and in the meantime I reflected on the news he'd just given me. Presumably the dearth of provisions explained why Aldebaran had been so preoccupied when

I met him: it must have been a heavy responsibility, and no doubt he was planning contingency measures. I was certain the shortages were merely temporary: from what I'd seen of these people, a major crisis was sure to be averted. Nonetheless, a chink had been exposed in their armour which Isabella and the others would have found most heartening. A feeling of exuberance swept over me as I dwelt on this thought, but it soon faded when I remembered Isabella's abrupt departure.

Plainly Yadegarian didn't trust me to mind the toast, because all of a sudden he came rushing back with a spoon in one hand and a dish in the other.

'Watch out!' he cried.

'Don't worry,' I said, quickly removing the pan from the grill. 'I've got it all under control.'

In fact, the toast was a little overdone for Yadegarian's liking. He gazed at it in despair for several long seconds, then gave a sigh and began slicing another loaf of bread.

'Help yourself to that lot,' he murmured. 'I can't serve it to our people: they're far too fussy.'

'Oh, thanks,' I said. 'Got any butter?'

Yadegarian ceased work and gave me a penetrating look.

'I told you the cupboard was bare,' he said. 'The butter ran out days ago.'

Yadegarian may have been a novice when it came to digging trenches, but here in the kitchen he was firmly in charge. It occurred to me I was probably being less of a help than a hindrance, so I took some toast, along with my dish and spoon, thanked him again and made a swift exit.

Up in the north, beyond the embankment, I noticed that Brigant's tent no longer stood alone. Seemingly, a few members of Hartopp's party had decided to move inland from the north-east, and there were now three or four angular tents arrayed across the slope. I was surprised that none of them had penetrated further south, where the grass grew thicker and richer, the terrain was more favourable, and the rain (according to local belief) less frequent. It was a golden opportunity, yet they all chose to stay away.

Hartopp himself was plainly going nowhere. His three upturned boats were marooned in a huge clump of nettles which virtually hid them from view. As a consequence, he and his sons hadn't been near them in weeks. The boats were out of commission for the foreseeable future, and it was Hartopp's stated intention to leave them exactly where they were (he said he liked the way they blended in with the foliage). Elsewhere, the forces of nature were equally hard at work. The embankment, for example, was gradually being enveloped by a sward of fresh greenery, with new shoots appearing every day over its entire length. Other parts of the field were dotted with thistles and similar species, while reeds and rushes continued to flourish at the water's edge.

It had been a long and bountiful summer. Even so, I had a feeling that change was on the way.

One evening at sunset I heard the familiar call of the bugle. I peered into the south-east and watched as people began lining up for their supper. It was a scene I'd witnessed on many previous occasions. Generally at meal times the camp ran like clockwork and queues tended to move fairly swiftly. Tonight, however, progress seemed rather sluggish. The cause of the delay was unclear, but I vaguely recalled Yadegarian telling me the cupboard was bare. I'd taken this to be a figure of speech, but perhaps it was nearer the truth than I realized. If so, then it was quite possible supper had been cancelled. By now the light was fading rapidly and there was little to be seen through the encroaching gloom. I listened attentively. Faint voices of protest could be heard in the distance, then they faded away as presumably the queue dispersed and people retired to their tents.

Suddenly a lone figure emerged from the shadows at the far side of the crossing. I knew at a glance who it was: whenever Eamont had an urgent message he always rushed along, bent forward in his haste to carry the news. Now, as he returned from his assignment, I sensed that important events were about to unfold and come to fruition. Without even pausing, Eamont entered the water and waded towards the Great Field. Once ashore, he headed for the encampment, where he was quickly lost from view.

My premonition proved to be correct. A short while later, blazing torches began moving around in the south-east, accompanied by a series of shouted commands and responses. Apparently the populace was being mobilized for some purpose or other. The sound of frenetic activity persisted throughout the hours of darkness, but not until morning was its full extent revealed. When dawn arrived I looked out of my doorway and saw the whole camp reduced to practically nothing. All the tents had been packed up ready for transportation; in fact, the leading columns were already on the move. Long trains of men carrying baggage and equipment forded the river and headed slowly southward. The exodus was observed in silence by Aldebaran. He stood motionless at the edge of his former dominion as the flags were lowered and his subordinates trudged away. It was a forlorn spectacle. The once-mighty citadel had been reduced to an area of flattened grass in the corner of the field, and I wondered what could have brought about such a hurried withdrawal.

After a few minutes I was joined by Hen, and together we watched the last stages being enacted. By this time only a dozen or so stragglers remained in the south-east; these included Aldebaran's personal attendants, a few of the handmaidens, and Eamont. Also present were Yadegarian and the other cooks. Their belongings were stacked close by, but they appeared to be in no rush to leave. Instead, they waited until Aldebaran had ended his lonely vigil; then Yadegarian approached him cautiously. There followed a prolonged conversation, after which heads were nodded and handshakes exchanged. Finally, Aldebaran peered westward and spotted me and Hen. He spoke briefly to Eamont, then came strolling in our direction.

'Morning,' he said, when he drew near. 'You'll have gathered by now that we're clearing out.'

'Yes,' I said. 'Any particular reason?'

'Several actually,' said Aldebaran in a weary tone, 'but the upshot is we need to return to headquarters fairly soon.'

'Oh,' I said, with surprise, 'I always assumed this was your headquarters.'

'No, no,' came the reply, 'this is little more than a mere outpost in a far-flung province.'

He went on to explain that running the camp had generated untold costs and expenses. It had been a burden on their resources which they could really do without under the current circumstances. Therefore, they'd decided simply to cut their losses and leave.

'I'm afraid we've rather overreached ourselves,' he concluded.

While Aldebaran was talking I gazed across at the embankment so recently completed by me, Yadegarian and the rest of the cooks. Casually I pondered whether this counted as a 'cost' or an 'expense'. I didn't say anything though: Aldebaran seemed to be in a melancholy mood and I had no wish to make it worse.

Over in the south-east, the cooks and the attendants

were busily reorganizing some of the baggage. When Aldebaran noticed the flurry of activity it must have triggered a secondary line of thought. Next moment he turned and addressed Hen, who'd been standing quietly nearby.

'I understand you were here before anyone else,' said Aldebaran. 'In the west, I mean.'

'Oh . . . er . . . yes,' replied Hen. 'Yes, I was.'

He appeared thoroughly taken aback by the remark, as if he'd forgotten his long-standing claim.

'The reason I mention it,' continued Aldebaran, 'is because we're leaving a small detachment behind. Some of the cooks and handmaidens have requested release from service, and this has been granted. It leaves us with fewer mouths to feed. We've also allowed them two or three tents which were surplus to requirements; and a small proportion of the remaining provisions.'

'What's it all got to do with me?' Hen enquired.

'Well,' said Aldebaran, 'they've expressed a desire to settle in the south-west, so they'd be bordering your territory.'

'I see.'

'Obviously, we wouldn't sanction it without your permission. So, do you have any objections?'

'No, of course not,' said Hen. 'They're most welcome.'

'Then maybe you could keep an eye on them until they're established?'

'Certainly.'

'Good,' said Aldebaran. 'That's most satisfactory.'

As it happened, the cooks and handmaidens had already begun their move to the south-west. They walked slowly in single file, carrying their few possessions, and every now and again we could hear excited voices drifting on the breeze. Meanwhile, Aldebaran's attendants had collected the last of the baggage and were now waiting for him by the crossing.

He was about to depart when I remembered I had a question of my own.

'Before you go,' I said, 'could you resolve a debate that's been raging amongst the rest of us?'

'I'll try,' said Aldebaran. 'What's it about?'

'The earthwork,' I said. 'We wondered whether its purpose was drainage or defence?'

Aldebaran did not need to consider his answer.

'Both,' he replied.

With that, he gave each of us a cursory nod before turning towards the crossing. His men watched his approach, then they all waded to the other side and set off in brisk pursuit of the baggage train. I noticed that none of them looked back as they left the Great Field behind them. Gradually they gained on their retreating comrades, and soon they were all dwindling into the distant haze. The last we heard of them was the plaintive call of the bugle, and then they were gone.

Over in the south-east something was glaring in the sunshine. The harsh, reflected light had an unnatural quality which made its source impossible to identify, so eventually Hen and I went to investigate. Only when we got closer did we realize what it was: the great copper bath lay abandoned on its side.

'Obviously surplus to requirements,' commented Hen.

'Yes,' I agreed. 'No use without hot water.'

With its splayed copper feet and elegantly curved rim, the bath was an excellent piece of workmanship. All the same, it made a sorry sight. It had been brought here especially as a gift for Isabella, yet she'd rejected it and gone her own way. Now it seemed little more than a worthless folly, serving only to remind me of the chances I'd missed.

After a couple of days, I decided to call on Yadegarian and his fellow settlers in the south-west. They'd chosen a spot at the furthermost turn of the river, and the difference between this and their former dwelling was quite a revelation. I was immediately impressed by the way they'd used leaves and grasses to transform their dull, buff-coloured tents into garlanded bowers. Additional decorations were provided by colourful bunting. The setting was very pleasant, and they were all delighted with their good fortune. Even so, they were hardly living in the lap of luxury. Yadegarian showed me the provisions they'd been allocated: these consisted entirely of biscuits from the emergency reserve. He offered me one to sample, and I noticed it was imprinted with the letter J.

'Ah, yes,' said Yadegarian. 'It must have come from the very bottom of the stash.'

'Did you bake it?' I enquired.

'We baked all of them,' he replied. 'Biscuits are our speciality.'

Despite its apparent vintage, the biscuit was delicious. Actually, in size, shape and texture it was remarkably similar to Hartopp's biscuits, and it occurred to me that in terms of cuisine the two parties had much in common. This gave me an idea: perhaps if they engaged with one another it would help to reduce the sense of division which had lately befallen the Great Field. I made a mental note to discuss the subject with Hen.

Such thoughts were for the future, of course. Meanwhile, the prime concern was the empty space created by Aldebaran's departure. Apart from the unwanted bath, the south-east now lay empty and desolate. Nevertheless, it would only be a matter of time before the whole region was up for grabs again. Personally, I had no wish to discourage newcomers, but I knew that some of my neighbours were less tolerant. To forestall another incursion, therefore, I made the suggestion that one of our own number should seize the unoccupied land.

'It's a golden opportunity for somebody,' I said. 'The views of the river are outstanding.'

Regrettably, there were no takers. Brigant was determined to remain north of the 'turf wall' (as he called it), and Hartopp felt that his stranded boats tied him to the north-east. Not even his sons were interested, although I often saw them roaming the deserted river bank. They told me they were looking for adventure, but ultimately they decided the lowlands were too tame for them.

Once again I was the only contender. The rich pastures were mine for the taking, and I had to confess the temptation was hard to resist. At the back of my mind, however, a doubt was lurking. Experience told me that whoever held the south-east soon became the object of intense scrutiny by the rest of the field. This was an inescapable truth, brought about by a combination of factors ranging from curiosity to outright envy, and I wasn't sure whether I welcomed the prospect. Consequently, I deferred making any move for the time being. I didn't rule it out entirely, but I decided I should at least sleep on it.

That was the plan, anyway.

As it turned out, sleep was rather hard to come by. In the dead of night I was awoken by a harsh clanging noise which seemed to emanate from the empty quarter. Quickly I put on my boots and went outside. I could see nothing in the darkness, but the clanging persisted in sporadic bursts, accompanied by assorted shouts and curses. The sounds I heard were strange and unfamiliar, and I was beginning to feel uneasy about the situation when suddenly an angry voice cried, 'Hey!'

The clanging ceased immediately.

The voice I recognized as belonging to Hartopp, and in a moment he appeared silhouetted on top of the embankment. Beside him were two other figures who I assumed to be Hollis and Eldred.

After a brief pause the clanging resumed again, only to be silenced by a further cry of 'Hey!'

There followed a chorus of derisive hoots and catcalls. These faded into the distance as the clamour gradually subsided. Intermittent blasts of wind continued to beat against my tent, but there was nothing else. The disturbance, apparently, was over.

In the morning I asked Hartopp what had happened.

'We had some visitors,' he replied. 'Men in boats.'

'That was quite a din they were making.'

'They were hammering the copper bath,' said Hartopp. 'Trying to break it up, I suppose.'

'Until you scared them off.'

'Yes.'

Presently we were joined by Brigant, then the three of us wandered down to the south-east to inspect the bath. Apart from a number of dents, I was pleased to note there was little obvious damage. If the raiders had been trying to extract value from the copper, they'd plainly gone the wrong way about it.

'They could keep hammering all day long and get nowhere,' I remarked. 'You can't break copper into pieces.'

'I wonder if they knew the bath's real purpose?' said Brigant.

'To judge by appearances, probably not,' said Hartopp. 'You saw them, then?'

'Only vaguely, I admit, but I can tell you just who they

were. I caught a glimpse of their boats when they were sailing away and I realized I'd seen them before. They're inveterate marauders from the distant north, led by a man called Hogust. We encountered them when we were travelling downriver.'

'Did we?' said Brigant. 'I don't remember that.'

'It was before you came aboard,' said Hartopp. 'Don't forget, the river has many tributaries.'

'Ah, yes.'

'This Hogust is a born menace, actually. I could hear him egging them all on last night.'

'Do you think they'll try again?' I asked.

'Not sure,' Hartopp replied. 'It depends what mood they're in.'

'Maybe they'll come and settle in the south-east.'

'Maybe,' said Hartopp, 'but again I'm not sure. They're not really the types to settle in any one place for very long: it's just as likely they'll go back upriver.'

'Well, let's hope they do,' said Brigant. 'We don't want them landing here.'

For a while we stood gazing at the horizon in silent speculation, then we all returned to the sanctuary of our tents. For my part, I'd found Hartopp's description of the raiders rather disquieting, and clearly Brigant felt the same way. As I mentioned earlier, I had absolutely nothing against newcomers; indeed, they often brought a wealth of variety and colour to the field, Isabella being a perfect example. There were certain limits, however, which Hogust and his comrades had patently exceeded. To arrive in the dead of night armed with hammers was wholly unacceptable, especially when people were trying to sleep. If this was how they behaved, then they definitely wouldn't be welcome, and I knew I wasn't alone in this sentiment.

The abandoned bath, of course, was an open invitation for further trouble. As long as it lay exposed for all to see then it was bound to attract unwanted attention, and I spent some time pondering what could be done. In the event, though, it was Yadegarian who provided a solution. Around mid-afternoon I spotted him leading a small party towards the south-east. When they reached the bath they gave it a thorough examination; then they began hauling it back the way they'd come. It was evidently quite heavy and they had a bit of a struggle. Nonetheless, they persevered until they got it home.

I assumed that Yadegarian had learnt about the raid and decided to take the bath into his safekeeping. This was a worthy deed, but in all probability it was destined to be forgotten. The bath would doubtless remain neglected in some obscure part of the field, surrounded by nettles and corroded by the elements, until it was totally lost from memory. An unfortunate fate, yet more or less inevitable. I was surprised, therefore, when Yadegarian set to work restoring it to its former glory. For hour after hour, he and his companions carefully hammered out the dents with wooden mallets; then they burnished the copper to a lustrous sheen. Finally, they placed the bath on an earthen pedestal in the centre of the camp. There it rested, gleaming in the sunshine.

Hen and I observed the entire process from start to finish. It was a fascinating spectacle, but later I discovered that Hen harboured deep misgivings. During the next few days he kept his promise to Aldebaran, dutifully watching over the settlers and making sure that all was well. As with everything else, he took the task very seriously. Even so, he was completely baffled by their obsession with the copper bath.

'I can't fathom them out,' he told me. 'They polish it over and over again, morning, noon and night.'

'Perhaps they're drawn to its unnatural splendour,' I suggested. 'After all, it's a fine piece of workmanship.'

'That's as may be,' said Hen, 'but it's still a worry as far as I'm concerned. They really ought to be busy preparing for the end of the season, conserving their supplies, gathering fuel and so forth. Instead, they pass their evenings dancing around that blessed bath.'

'Lucky them,' I said. 'Sounds like a pleasant enough pastime.'

'It's no laughing matter,' he retorted. 'Summer won't last for ever.'

'No, I suppose not.'

'They should at least be baking fresh biscuits.'

Hen's comments reminded me of the idea I'd been considering.

'Oh, by the way,' I said, 'talking of biscuits . . .'

It was as far as I got.

All at once, a commotion erupted in the north-east. We heard a warning shout from Hartopp, and the next moment a number of long, narrow sailing boats came sweeping down the river. Immediately, Yadegarian's people rushed to the copper bath and concealed it beneath a tarpaulin; then they retired to their tents. Meanwhile, the boats reached the south-east corner and several men scrambled ashore. Another group stayed afloat, as if primed for a swift getaway. It seemed the raiders had returned, and on this occasion they'd arrived in broad daylight.

We watched the landing party as they scoured the area where the bath had previously lain. When they realized it was gone they stood staring blankly at the empty ground; obviously this was something they hadn't bargained for. A delay followed, after which we heard instructions being barked from one of the boats. At such a distance we couldn't tell what was being said, but the meaning soon became clear. Within minutes, all the boats had been pulled onto the bank and their sails dropped; then everyone started unloading tents and equipment. Everyone, that is, except the man giving the orders. He was a stocky fellow with a gruff voice, and was the very last to come ashore.

'Hogust, I presume,' said Hen.

'Yes,' I said. 'He must have decided to stay after all.'

'Perhaps it's only temporary.'

'Yes, perhaps.'

We continued to watch while Hogust surveyed his new surroundings. The men under his command were an undisciplined bunch. They were wandering about in a haphazard manner, apparently choosing places to pitch their tents, then changing their minds again. Two or three, I noticed, were squabbling over some items of baggage. They pushed and shoved one another with voices raised, and looked as if they were about to come to blows. Next instant, however, the dispute dissolved into raucous laughter. A couple of playful punches were thrown, and that was the end of it.

Hogust, in the meantime, had taken several paces away from his rowdy associates. He was now standing alone, peering at the vacant swathe of grass that lay before him. Evidently something had caught his attention. All of a sudden he turned on his heels and rejoined the others, snapping out a new set of instructions. A howl of protest rose up, but Hogust silenced it by cuffing the ear of the man nearest to him. After that, they all did as they were told. With their leader urging them to get a move on, they quickly reloaded the boats and hoisted the sails. Finally, they pushed off and headed back upriver.

Hen and I witnessed the undignified withdrawal in astonishment.

'What's caused that, I wonder?' said Hen.

'Not sure,' I replied. 'Let's go and have a look.'

We made certain the visitors had properly gone, then strolled over to the south-east. It was eerily quiet, and there was nothing to suggest that only ten minutes earlier a horde of unruly men had been roving all over the place. The only signs of habitation were those left by Aldebaran and his people. During the past week, the flattened grass had begun to make a partial recovery. Nonetheless, we could plainly see the impressions left by a multitude of tents. They stretched away in every direction and told the story of a huge force recently departed. The vision they conjured up must have unnerved Hogust; hence his rapid retreat.

The truth, of course, was slightly different: the impressions in the grass were the last traces of a fading power that was unlikely ever to return. If he'd so chosen, Hogust could have stayed where he was for as long as he wished. Unfortunately for him, he seemed to have been ambushed by his own imagination.

Even so, the incident had demonstrated yet again the need for a permanent presence in the south-east. Ideally, it required a person of substance to fulfil the role: someone whose natural gravitas expressed their irrefutable right to be there; someone whose tent was majestic rather than showy; grand but not overbearing. Only when this was achieved would the other residents feel less imposed upon, and only then would outsiders like Hogust be dissuaded from chancing their luck.

As it transpired, we hadn't seen the last of that

character. The following morning his boats landed in the north-east, and again the men brought their baggage ashore. They completely ignored Hartopp, who was watching from a short distance away; then, without a 'by your leave', they began setting up camp right next door to him. Needless to say, they didn't go about this task quietly: it appeared every move, however small, entailed a stream of shouting, horseplay and general rowdiness. Bedecked with barbaric pennants, their tents were garish and ugly. They pitched them side-by-side and back-to-back, all jammed together with hardly a space in between. It was a tight squeeze, and by the time they'd finished they were practically butting up against Hartopp's meticulously ordered encampment.

Understandably, Hartopp was appalled but, as he later remarked, there was nothing he could do. Hogust and his confederates had as much right to be in the field as anybody else.

'We've no choice,' said Hartopp in a resigned tone. 'I'm afraid we'll just have to learn to live with them.'

Why Hogust decided to settle so close by was anybody's guess. The only explanation I could think of was that he'd seen Hartopp's upturned boats and recognized him as a fellow sailor. All the same, the notion of going and introducing himself seemed not to have entered Hogust's head. Instead, once established, he started poking around the area, presumably in search of plunder. At one stage he barged into the clump of nettles, apparently insensitive to their stings, and studied the three boats in detail. He tapped their hulls and prodded their keels for signs of rot, then ran his hands over the paintwork as though contemplating whether it was worthwhile salvaging the vessels. I could have told him they were in superb condition (they were bound to be, knowing Hartopp) but that was beside the point. Obviously Hogust had no concept of private property; and it was equally obvious that Hartopp would need to keep a sharp eye on him.

In the meantime, some of the crew had forayed inland. Eventually, they encountered the trench crossing their path. It, too, was now full of burgeoning nettles, but undeterred they jumped across and climbed onto the grassy embankment. There they stood gazing into the south, but for some reason they ventured no further. I could see them clearly from my tent, and I noticed they all had jutting brows. They grinned at me for a moment or two, and I nodded in acknowledgement; then they went back the way they'd come. Seemingly, they'd roamed far enough for the present.

It was difficult to tell if they were going to be a perpetual nuisance, or whether they would quieten down after a day or two. Sadly, the forecasts were not encouraging. To judge by the constant racket they made, they had absolutely no consideration for the people living around them. Nor was there any let-up when darkness fell: the noise persisted throughout the evening as they caroused and argued on the river bank. I lay awake in my tent and reflected on the peaceful life we'd known long ago, before the advent of strident bugles, tuneless clanging and boisterous laughter, when the only sound had been the gentle stirring of the wind. Those days were now remote indeed.

Ultimately, however, even Hogust and his men required sleep. Sometime after midnight they went to bed and silence descended over the field at last. For a while I continued listening, just to make sure there was nobody on the prowl. As a matter of fact I did hear something: a kind of distant murmuring, or perhaps a whirring of wings; but then it, too, subsided. I pondered the question of the newcomers and realized that Hartopp was probably correct: we would simply have to learn to live with them. Finally, I sank into a deep sleep.

In the morning I was slowly awoken by the sunlight filtering through my canvas walls. All was quiet, and I assumed the longboatmen were still at their slumbers. The height of the sun told me I'd slept much later than usual, so after a few more minutes I roused myself and got up. I unfastened my doorway, then peered outside and beheld a shimmering white tent in the south-east.

Blinking with disbelief I looked again, but I was not mistaken. The tent stood in exactly the same place as it had before, dominating the river and perfectly befitting its lush surroundings. Moreover, it still retained its air of timelessness, so that it appeared to have been there for ever, rather than only a few hours. The tent's magnificence was beyond compare. Splendid and gracious in equal measure, it bestowed a certain tranquillity upon the Great Field, and for these reasons I welcomed its return.

Even so, my feelings were tempered when the doorway parted and Thomas emerged. As usual he was barefoot, bearded, and dressed in flowing white robes. He paused a moment, and I waited for him to glance around the field in his usual all-encompassing manner. Instead, though, he turned and addressed someone inside the tent. This I found rather perplexing because in the past he'd always travelled alone; indeed, his self-regard was so inflated that I wouldn't have thought he needed any companionship.

I watched with mounting interest as the conversation continued. Thomas was now standing fairly close to the entrance, his shoulders hunched and his arms outstretched, and gradually I realized that it was not so much a conversation as an argument. Furthermore, to judge by his awkward stance, Thomas seemed to be losing. The person inside the tent clearly had him on the ropes, and casually I wondered what he could have done to deserve such disapprobation. Perhaps if he'd raised his voice a little I could have picked up a few details, but to his credit Thomas remained calm and merely shrugged in a gesture of apparent defeat. Next moment he headed towards the crossing. I had no idea whether he saw me peering out from the recess of my tent; if he did, he gave no indication, but I sensed that he'd rather nobody had witnessed his discomfiture. Accordingly, I withdrew slightly into the shadows.

When Thomas reached the crossing I expected him to enter the water and head directly for the opposite side, as he had done so many times in the past. Today, however, he stopped abruptly at the bank and stood gazing into the south. There was nothing to be seen. Apart from a few scattered trees, the fields beyond the river were quite empty, yet Thomas continued to scrutinize the horizon. I surmised, therefore, that he must be waiting for someone. Whoever it was, they were plainly overdue. The sun was gaining height with the approach of midday, but still nobody appeared. For his part, Thomas was becoming increasingly impatient. He paced back and forth on the river bank, occasionally casting a glance towards the shimmering white tent, then turning to resume his vigil once again.

By now, though, I was paying scant attention to Thomas and his concerns. During the course of the morning, fresh eruptions had occurred in the north-east as Hogust's comrades greeted another day. An endless series of bangs and crashes shattered the peace, so eventually I decided to wander over and give Hartopp some moral support. I made my way through the chaotic ranks of tents to his beleaguered settlement and found him carrying out a daily inspection. Evidently, he was trying his best to adhere to his routine, but it was no easy task with fights and squabbles breaking out every few minutes. So far his property had survived unscathed, but Hartopp confessed his nerves were beginning to jangle. Indeed, he was so distracted that he'd only just noticed the return of the shimmering white tent. It was a fact he observed with dismay.

'I was hoping Hogust would move to the south-east,' he said. 'Little chance of that now.'

Further up the river bank, several longboats had been drawn ashore. Their sails were fully rigged as if in readiness for a forthcoming raid, but actually they were going nowhere.

'They're forever putting up their sails and taking them down again,' explained Hartopp. 'Must be force of habit.'

Among the men standing around the longboats I could see Hollis and Eldred. They seemed totally absorbed by the spectacle, and quite at ease in the company of strangers. I viewed this as a positive sign for future integration. Hartopp, on the other hand, was less optimistic.

'Bound to be a bad influence,' he remarked. 'I don't want my boys setting off downriver on some sortie.'

'No,' I said. 'I doubt if you do.'

'Probably never see them again.'

'No.'

Clearly, Hartopp's policy of learning to live with the newcomers had its limitations, so I thought it wise to change the subject.

'By the way,' I said, 'I haven't seen Brigant lately.'

'No,' replied Hartopp, 'you won't have. He retired to his tent with a headache shortly after the longboats arrived.'

'Ah.'

'Could be days before he recovers.'

'Weeks more like, knowing Brigant.'

'Yes,' said Hartopp. 'Maybe.'

The disclosure made me smile to myself: henceforward, Brigant would have to be careful who he called 'soft'.

While we'd been talking, I'd noticed Hogust standing alone on the river bank. He'd already glanced our way once or twice, and now he came strolling purposefully towards us.

'Hello,' I murmured, as he approached. 'Looks as if he means business.'

Hogust didn't bother to introduce himself.

'Right,' he said, speaking directly to Hartopp. 'Proposition for you. One of my boats for one of yours.'

'Sorry,' Hartopp answered, 'they're not for sale.'

Hogust instantly adopted a pained expression.

'I didn't mention selling, did I?' he said. 'Did I mention selling? No, I didn't. I meant a straight swap.'

'Same answer,' said Hartopp. 'Sorry.'

Now Hogust turned to me.

'Straight swap's fair enough, isn't it?' he said. 'What do you think?'

'Well,' I said. 'Yes, I suppose it's fair in principle.'

At this point Hartopp glared at me as though I'd betrayed him, and I suddenly realized that Hogust was a wily operator who knew all the tricks in the book. Plainly he was trying to use me to probe Hartopp's defences. He was standing very close and peering at us from beneath his jutting brow; first at Hartopp, then at me, then at Hartopp again.

'Trouble is,' I added quickly, 'fairness doesn't enter into it.'

Hogust was obviously impressed by my words. For several moments he stared at the ground in silence, then finally he let out a sigh.

'Fairness doesn't enter into it,' he repeated. 'How's that for gratitude? I was only trying to do the man a favour.'

I had a feeling this comment was simply another trick in Hogust's repertoire; namely, an attempt to gain sympathy. Fortunately it didn't wash with Hartopp, who made it quite clear that negotiations were at an end.

'Thanks all the same,' he said, 'but no thanks.'

Hogust was apparently unaccustomed to being stood up to, and I could see that Hartopp had thereby earned his respect. Nevertheless, he wasn't finished yet.

'Tell you what,' he said, in a last flourish, 'I'll give you a few more days to think about it.'

Hartopp said nothing else, and for the next minute or so we all gazed idly at the distant white tent, shimmering in the south-east. It was partially obscured from view by the earthwork which divided the field so effectively, and which the northerners had labelled the 'turf wall'. In consequence, the white tent appeared to belong to another world entirely. Detached and remote, it stood in stark contrast to the crowded encampments of the north-east.

'That earthwork,' said Hogust, finally breaking the silence, 'blocks the way south, doesn't it?'

'Yes,' replied Hartopp. 'That's why it was built in the first place.'

'And for drainage,' I added.

'Drainage?' said Hogust. 'For whose benefit, exactly?'

'The people in the south-east,' I said, 'although it's still to be tried and tested.'

'Why?'

'There's been no rain since the job was completed.'

'I see.'

'All that talk about drainage was just an excuse,' declared Hartopp. 'The real purpose was to keep the rest of us out.'

'That's what it looks like to me,' agreed Hogust. 'A defensive rampart.'

'But it doesn't go right across the field,' I protested. 'You can easily skirt it in the west.'

'Maybe so,' said Hogust, 'but at the end of the day a wall's still a wall.'

'Of course it is,' said Hartopp.

There was a brief pause in the conversation, during which Hogust stared thoughtfully at the earthwork.

'What it really needs,' he said at length, 'is a sally port here and there.'

Hartopp nodded his approval, and it struck me that an affinity was beginning to develop between him and Hogust. I had no idea what a sally port was, but I guessed it must be some kind of opening or breach in the embankment. Soon the pair of them were discussing the best way to approach the task, and I realized that with so many men at their disposal it could be readily accomplished. Whether talk would evolve into action was a different question altogether. I left them making their plans and headed for home.

I'd been gone for a good hour, so I was surprised to see that Thomas was still down at the crossing, gazing southward. The doorway of his tent, meanwhile, remained firmly closed. I found the situation totally baffling, so eventually I went over and asked Hen what he made of it all.

'Beats me,' he said. 'I've been watching Thomas all afternoon and he hasn't once deserted his post.'

'Must be expecting somebody important,' I ventured.

'Yes, probably,' said Hen, 'although I can't imagine who.'

'Me neither.'

Hen's tent was standing nearby, and I noticed that during the past few days he'd added an extra flysheet.

'This dry spell can't last for ever,' he remarked, by way of explanation. 'We're due a downpour very soon.'

Hen had made similar utterances ever since I'd known him, and I was quite used to his seasonal predictions. Generally I paid them little heed because it was more or less impossible to forecast the weather in the Great Field. Today, however, Hen's earnest tone of voice suggested his gloomy outlook might just be correct. I realized I'd made no preparations whatsoever for the onset of autumn, and I determined to deal with the matter over the next few days. As I pondered all this, Hen reached into his tent and produced a tin box.

'Like a biscuit?' he asked.

'Oh, yes, please,' I replied. 'I didn't know you had any.'

'They're a recent acquisition.'

The biscuit he offered me was familiar in size, shape and texture, and was imprinted with the letter J.

'Aha,' I said. 'I've seen these before.'

'Thought you might have,' said Hen. 'I traded them with Yadegarian for some supplies.'

'Good idea.'

'Hopefully it'll encourage him to bake some more.'

Hen closed the tin box and put it away.

'Do you mind if I save this for later?' I enquired.

'Of course not,' he said. 'Be my guest.'

After thanking him again, I returned to my tent and stored the biscuit in a safe place (next to my dish and spoon).

Down at the crossing, Thomas's long wait seemed to be coming to an end. He'd ceased pacing back and forth and was now peering fixedly into the distance. I followed the line of his gaze, and after a few moments I spotted a troop of men advancing from the south, all laden with baggage. Immediately, Thomas entered the water and waded over to meet them. He appeared quite tense, as if uncertain of the new arrivals, and as they gathered around him I couldn't help thinking how large they all were. He greeted two of them with cautious handshakes and they held a brief discussion; then he turned and led the entire troop towards the Great Field. By now the light was beginning to fade, but when they neared the bank I could clearly see that they were all wearing iron helmets. After a further word from Thomas, they removed these and stowed them away.

Something else caught my attention too. Amongst the heavy baggage I noticed two or three rather delicate items. A strange sensation passed through me as I recognized an eiderdown (tied with silk cord), a tapestry (wrapped in ticking), and a collection of velvet cushions (loose).

With darkness falling, Thomas directed his guests to the south-east and they started setting up camp. Meanwhile, at the far side of the embankment, Hogust's people resumed their revelries, apparently oblivious to the newcomers. It was the usual story: a constant stream of disturbances that continued late into the evening. I could still hear them cavorting in the moonlight when I went to bed.

Needless to say I endured a very restless night, and on this occasion it wasn't Hogust keeping me awake. The sight of Isabella's belongings had left me wondering where she could be, while at the same time guessing the probable answer. Finally, at dawn, I gave up trying to sleep and went outside. Over in the south-east, a ring of tents surrounded Thomas's effulgent dwelling. There was no sign of Thomas; nor could I see Hen or any of the others. For the time being I had the field completely to myself, so I decided to make the most of the peace and quiet.

One thing was definite: I had no intention of being excluded from any part of the field simply because Thomas had chosen to return. I was free to roam wherever I wanted; therefore, I sauntered across to have a closer look at the newly pitched tents. Their occupants were presumably asleep inside, so I approached stealthily and gave them a thorough examination. The nearest tent was cream and turquoise in colour, with steep walls and a pointed roof. The next was orange and purple. To judge by its rather 'weathered' condition it was very well-travelled, and I imagined it had been employed on countless expeditions to faraway places. The edge of the roof was encircled by an ornate fringe, and from its peak flew a forked pennant. I noticed this had an unusual design, so I stood on tiptoe to try and get a better view. Next instant somebody grabbed my ankles, my feet were jerked from under me and I fell flat on my face. Quickly my arms were pinioned behind my back; then I felt my assailant's knee bearing down on my neck. I was completely unable to move, and I could scarcely breathe.

A few seconds passed, and then a voice spoke quietly in my ear. 'Not planning to stick your nose into my affairs, are you?'

When I failed to answer, the knee was pressed down harder, so eventually I shook my head.

'Does that mean "no"?'

I managed a nod.

'Good,' said the voice. 'In future, I don't want any

comments, meddling or interference. You must understand that what I do and where I go is none of your business. Now, have you got the message?'

I nodded once more, and at last I was allowed to breathe again. The pressure was removed from my neck and my arms were released, but for a while I remained lying face down in the grass. I was in a mild state of shock, partly because of the casual violence, and partly because the voice belonged to Isabella.

'Come on,' she said at length. 'Stand up.'

'Alright,' I answered. 'Give me a chance.'

I got slowly to my feet and brushed myself down before glancing around the field.

'Don't worry,' said Isabella. 'There's nobody watching.'

She was clad all in crimson, and stood eyeing me with her hands on her hips.

'How did you do that?' I asked. 'You're smaller than me.'

'I've learned a few things on my travels,' she replied.

'So you thought you'd teach me a lesson.'

'Correct.'

'Even though I haven't done anything.'

'Not yet, no,' she said, 'but your track record is hardly encouraging. Let's call it a preventative strike.'

Inside the tent, there was a loud grunt followed by a yawn. Somebody had just woken up, so Isabella put her finger to her lips and we moved away a short distance.

'Right,' she said. 'I'll leave you to your exploits and I'll continue with my own. Our paths needn't cross again.'

'Is this your final decision?' I enquired.

Isabella gazed at me and shook her head sadly, but she had nothing further to add. Instead, she turned and walked silently away. As I watched her go, I debated the possibility that she actually meant the opposite of what she said; that she'd subjected me to a kind of 'rough wooing' with the promise of better things to come. My hopes were dashed, however, when she reached the shimmering white tent and slipped gracefully inside.

Meanwhile, the grunts and yawns were getting louder and more persistent, so I walked briskly to the river bank and followed it all the way round to the west. I was just passing Hen's tent when he came out and wished me a good morning. I could barely bring myself to reply, but I murmured some nicety and together we stood looking towards the south-east.

'I see Thomas has company,' Hen remarked.

I presumed he was referring to the new tents, but I couldn't be sure. Hen often knew more than he let on.

'Yes,' I said. 'Arrived late yesterday afternoon.'

'"Late" being the operative word,' said Hen. 'No wonder Thomas was pacing up and down so much.'

By now, the sun had fully risen. All across the field we could hear the sounds of another day beginning, and in due course Thomas emerged from the shimmering white tent. He was followed soon afterwards by Isabella.

'Good grief!' exclaimed Hen.

Evidently he'd been unaware of Isabella's presence,

and I had to admit it was odd that she'd kept such a low profile since returning. After all, she was hardly a shrinking violet. Suddenly, though, the answer occurred to me: she'd been waiting to be reunited with her personal effects. Not until the eiderdown, the tapestry and the velvet cushions were installed in their proper place would she be satisfied. I was coming to realize that what mattered most to Isabella was the inner tent, rather than the outer trappings.

Considering she'd only just moved in with him, Thomas was paying her remarkably little attention. He stood with his back to Isabella, gazing around the field in his customary manner, and eventually his eyes alighted on the embankment. Next moment, he went strolling over to inspect it more closely. I watched intrigued as he walked its length from east to west, casting critical glances here and there, and appraising the earthwork in general. By now it had begun to blend in fully with its surroundings: it was grassing over nicely, and I was proud of the part I'd played in its construction. Accordingly, the sight of Thomas taking a proprietorial interest annoyed me no end. True enough, he was the main beneficiary of the drainage scheme; yet surely all the organization, the hard graft, the misunderstandings and the disagreements weren't just so that he could swan around without getting his feet wet!

What the newcomers made of their enrobed and bearded host was anybody's guess. They were plainly here at Thomas's invitation, but they looked a formidable bunch, and somehow I couldn't picture them going barefoot through the pasture (heavy boots were much more likely). The exact purpose of their visit was far from clear, and as I gazed at their circle of tents I wondered how long they proposed to stay. There'd been no sign of them in the morning, so I assumed they were still resting after their arduous journey. Doubtless they'd surface sooner or later.

Over on the other side of the embankment, it was business as usual. Random shouts and yells signalled that Hogust's people were up and about and causing mayhem. Already I'd seen a few sails being hoisted on the river bank, only to be subsequently lowered again. This was typical of the way they lived. From what I'd observed, they were restive people who hadn't really got enough to do; therefore, they spent their time making a nuisance of themselves. Poor Hartopp acted as a sort of buffer zone, and to some extent he was a calming influence. Nonetheless, sooner or later they were bound to break out of the north-east and head southward: the temptation of the lush, open grassland was simply far too great.

Of course, there was one thing the northerners all had in common. Without exception, they viewed the earth-work as a defensive rampart. They saw it as a barrier between the upper and lower field, and the idea of creating an opening had already been mooted. I was unsure whether such a plan would improve relations or simply cause hostilities, especially in the light of recent developments, but I decided I should at least find out if any progress was being made. The last time I saw Hartopp and Hogust they'd been discussing the project in earnest, so with some urgency I set off for the north-east.

Halfway there I encountered Brigant. He'd seemingly put an end to his period of self-imposed confinement and was about to rejoin society. I didn't need to ask how he was feeling. His opening remark was both caustic and spiky: ample proof that he'd made a full recovery.

'He's come back then,' he said, 'our fairweather friend.'

'You mean Thomas?' I replied. 'Yes, it's been a couple of days now.'

'Never see him when it's raining, do we?' Brigant continued.

'No, I suppose not.'

'Nor when there's a howling gale.'

'No.'

'Like I said: fairweather friend.'

Obviously Brigant had lost touch with current affairs while he was laid up. His store of gossip was totally out of date, and he was due for a bit of a shock next time he peered into the south. I didn't say anything though: he'd find out for himself soon enough.

When I reached the north-east, I was pleased to discover that plans for breaching the embankment had been shelved. Hartopp and Hogust remained on cordial terms with one another, but they'd failed to agree who would be in charge of the operation. Actually, Hartopp had enough on his plate dealing with Hollis and Eldred. They pestered him unceasingly to let them take the boats so they could ply the river in search of adventure. So far he'd resisted their demands, but he wasn't sure if he could hold out much longer.

'They think life under sail is all fun and games,' he said. 'They've forgotten the hard slog when you have to come back upstream.'

Hogust, meanwhile, had made a further offer for Hartopp's vessels. Apparently he now wanted all three.

'Why's he so eager to get hold of them?' I enquired.

'Because his longboats are all worn out,' replied Hartopp. 'He's been sailing them for years.'

'What's on the table? Straight swap?'

'Yep.'

'But the answer's still "no".'

'Correct,' said Hartopp. 'I wasn't born yesterday.'

'Quite.'

'In any case, I need workhorses not jollyboats.'

He gave a weary sigh. Evidently he had much to contend with, and the strain was beginning to show. Apart from his worries over Hollis and Eldred, he was obliged to keep a constant watch over his turbulent neighbours. Thanks to Hogust and his crew, the entire north-east had drifted into a state of ferment. Hartopp was under pressure from all directions, and for this reason his decision to stand firm was all the more admirable.

'Oh, by the way,' he remarked, 'I noticed some new tents appeared overnight.'

'Actually they arrived late yesterday afternoon,' I said. 'Around dusk.'

I didn't mean to sound as if I was correcting Hartopp, but regrettably that was how it came out.

'Alright,' he said, in a flat tone of voice. 'Dusk then. It hardly makes any difference, does it?'

'It made a difference to Isabella,' I announced. 'They kept her waiting for hours.'

When he heard Isabella's name, Hartopp's eyes widened.

'She's back then?' he murmured.

'Yes,' I replied.

'Well, why didn't you mention it before?'

Now he had that betrayed look on his face again, and I realized I needed to choose my words even more carefully. At the back of my mind there also lurked Isabella's injunction, forbidding me from discussing her private affairs. I'd already gone too far, if the truth be told, but I didn't want to make matters any worse.

'I couldn't really,' I said. 'Not under the circumstances.'

Hartopp regarded me for a long moment, then turned and peered southward.

'Where's her crimson tent?' he asked. 'I can't see it.'

Again I was unable to answer.

Down in the south-east, a few of the newcomers were roaming around near the river bank. They moved slowly and purposefully, and had an air of quiet authority about them. Further away, at the very turn of the river, stood Thomas. He was talking to two of the men (they looked like the two he'd shaken hands with the previous day) and the discussion continued for some time. Meanwhile, Isabella emerged from the shimmering white tent and began a series of bending and stretching exercises.

Hartopp turned to face me. He'd gone rather pale.

'So she's with him?'

'Yes,' I said.

'Seems as if I'm the last to know,' he said solemnly. 'Just shows what she thinks of me, doesn't it?'

I gave no reply. Hartopp was plainly shaken by what he'd seen, so I desperately cast about for some way to distract him from his troubles. What I required was a subject close to his heart (apart from Isabella), and it occurred to me that I should have brought along the biscuit imprinted with the letter J. Over the past day or two, I'd been harbouring a vague notion about using it to demonstrate the similarity between the various settlements dotted across the field; and maybe even initiate some rudimentary trading. Naturally, Hartopp would have been a key player in such a project (he was, after all, a leading exponent of biscuits) but unfortunately I'd forgotten my sample. The opportunity was lost.

Just then, to cap it all, I saw Hogust strolling towards us.

'Not now, Hogust,' I thought to myself. 'Hartopp can probably do without your ceaseless badgering.'

In the event, however, Hogust provided exactly the kind of distraction I'd been seeking. Apparently he had yet another proposal for Hartopp.

'How would you like us to clear those nettles from around your boats?' he asked.

'No, thanks,' Hartopp answered.

'We'll do it free of charge,' Hogust added.

This was obviously a ploy to gain easier access to the vessels, but Hartopp was having none of it.

'I'll clear them in my own good time,' he said, 'thank you very much.'

Hogust tutted with exasperation, then he tried changing tack.

'Look, Hartopp,' he said, 'you don't really need your boats any more, so why not let me take them off your hands? I mean to say, you're nicely settled here and you've probably done with travelling.'

'Maybe so,' said Hartopp, 'but I'd prefer to keep my boats in reserve.'

'Whatever for?'

Hartopp didn't reply to this question. Instead, he went on the offensive.

'Besides,' he said, 'you're nicely settled here too. You must be. Whenever you prepare to leave, you change your mind at the last minute and take your sails down again.'

'That's our choice,' said Hogust. 'We're a nautical people. We come and go when we please.'

'Well, if you're a nautical people,' said Hartopp, 'why don't you build some new boats?'

For a few moments Hogust was rendered speechless by the observation. The look of surprise on his face suggested it had never occurred to him to build any vessels of his own. How he'd acquired his present, ageing fleet was known only to him, but judging by his predatory instincts I could hazard a fair guess.

'Of course, we could build some if we wanted to,' he spluttered, 'but we've rarely had the need.'

'It's fairly simple when you know what you're doing,' Hartopp added.

'Of course it is.'

'I could give you a hand if you like.'

'No, no,' said Hogust. 'Thanks anyway, but we've got plenty enough boats when I think about it.'

There was a movement beside me, and I realized that sometime during the conversation we'd been joined by Brigant. To get here he would have had to pass through Hogust's cluttered encampment, but clearly his distaste for the noise and squalor had been overcome by sheer curiosity. Now he stood peering with interest at the man with the jutting brow.

'You off then?' he asked.

'Hadn't planned on it,' Hogust replied. 'Depends on the weather.'

To my ears this sounded like an excuse for inaction. It was quite obvious Hogust wasn't going anywhere, but he refused to admit the fact (especially to himself). Moreover, to invoke the weather was completely spurious: a man of his experience should be able to sail in any conditions if he so desired. As it happened, there hadn't been a drop of rain since Aldebaran's hurried departure several weeks ago. Despite all prophesies, the Great Field remained dry. Consequently it was attractive to people who dwelt in tents, and these naturally included Hogust. Nevertheless, he continued the charade of being ready to leave at a moment's notice.

Hartopp, meanwhile, had given a very impressive performance. He'd channelled his disappointment over Isabella into a successful sparring match with Hogust, and he seemed all the better for it. Furthermore, he now had Brigant for reinforcement.

'I was thinking,' he remarked at length, 'that a few of us could move up to the north-west.'

'How do you mean?' enquired Hogust.

'Well,' said Hartopp, 'it's the only part of the field that's still unoccupied. Oh, I know it's a bit wild and windswept in that direction, but there's ample space for anyone who likes a challenge. Actually, I'm surprised nobody's settled there already.'

'Probably too harsh for most types,' adjoined Brigant. 'You'd need to be pretty resilient to last very long.'

'Really?' said Hogust.

He turned and peered into the north-west, with the dark hills rising in the distance beyond.

'A challenge, eh?' he murmured. 'Yes, I suppose it would be.'

Hartopp and Brigant plainly had the measure of Hogust. I left the three of them discussing the merits and pitfalls of a move to the north-west, and wandered homeward. There was no telling if Hartopp had truly set aside his feelings for Isabella, or whether he'd merely adopted a brave face. Either way, he was putting on a more convincing show than I could manage. I was sliding gradually into the depths of despond, and the matter wasn't helped when I glanced at the shimmering white tent. There, reposing beneath its ornate canopy, lay Thomas and Isabella, the afternoon sunlight bathing them in a soft, warm glow.

Now it was me who needed a distraction. I turned away and was glad to see Hen hovering casually near the river bank in the west. In general, Hen was the last person to hover casually, so I guessed he had some news to impart. I also sensed that it was not for public consumption. Adjusting my course, I advanced towards the river until our paths converged; then, without speaking, we strolled together along the bank. Not until we'd gone a good way did Hen break the silence. Apparently, during my absence, he'd received a courtesy visit from Thomas.

'Just turned up at my tent,' said Hen. 'Quite unexpected.'

'Yes,' I replied. 'Must have been.'

'He apologized for deserting the field at such a crucial juncture, but the fault lay wholly with Julian's people.'

'Oh yes?'

'It seems they treated Thomas very shoddily,' Hen continued. 'They lured him away under false pretences; then they used all kinds of tricks and obfuscation to delay his return.'

Once again I was struck by Thomas's overweening sense of self-importance. From what I could gather, he assumed the entire population had been waiting for him to come back and take up his former residence. Why he thought any of us should care one way or another was beyond me, but Hen was certainly indignant on his behalf.

'What were these false pretences?' I asked. 'Precisely?'

'It makes a sorry tale,' said Hen. 'Initially they tried to play down their interest in the Great Field and insisted they were "just looking". On close questioning, however, it soon became clear they had a speculative motive. They told Thomas they were also considering a number of similar options elsewhere; and as proof of their good faith they invited him to accompany them while they reviewed several other possibilities in the southern lands beyond the river. On the spur of the moment he agreed to go with them, but it was a decision he came to regret. In the course of the journey Julian was revealed to be a man of great ambition, and relations between him and Thomas eventually soured.'

'Ambition,' I said. 'Is that why Julian was overthrown?'

'Most probably,' answered Hen. 'Thereafter, Thomas

found life very difficult. Julian's successors claimed that nothing had changed and that he remained their honoured guest. In reality, though, he felt as if he was being held hostage: he was friendless and far from home, and only after a long struggle did he manage to break free of them.'

Hen paused and glanced into the south-east.

'The upshot of all this,' he announced, 'is that Thomas no longer trusts anybody, which is why he enlisted the services of Horsefall and Griep.'

'The people who arrived last night?'

'Yes,' said Hen. 'By all accounts they're seasoned campaigners.'

'They look like thugs to me.'

'Well, Hogust looks like a thug,' Hen replied, 'but you seem to have made friends with him alright.'

'That's different,' I said. 'Hogust's based in the north-east, whereas this lot are practically next door.'

Hen gave a shrug.

'If you don't like it,' he said, 'you'll just have to move somewhere else, won't you?'

Evidently, Hen was prepared to brook no criticism of Thomas's judgement. I found his perpetual loyalty quite inexplicable, but there was no point in arguing with him. Even so, I still had my doubts. As we resumed our stroll, I debated whether Thomas hadn't made a grave error. After all, Horsefall and Griep could hardly be described as meek and mild retainers: on the contrary, they were heavyweights who'd arrived with a band of equally heavy accomplices. True enough, their circle of tents was likely to discourage anyone else from settling nearby, and perhaps this was just what Thomas wanted. Nonetheless, I wondered at what cost his splendid isolation had been achieved.

Presently, our stroll took us to the extreme south-west of the field. Here we encountered a very pleasant scene: Yadegarian and his followers peacefully decorating their bowers, baking biscuits and tending the copper bath. Hen was rather pleased about the biscuits, especially since they'd acted on his advice and replenished their stocks.

'We regard you as a sort of father figure,' Yadegarian told him. 'You're welcome here whenever you wish.'

'Thanks,' Hen replied, glancing all around him. 'I must confess, you seem to have created a perfect settlement.'

Indeed, the contrast with the hubbub of the north-east was striking. Instead of tumult, there was tranquillity; instead of fights and squabbles, there was harmony. At the same time, I couldn't help noticing the air of vulnerability that lay over the camp. Kindness and hospitality were all very well, but they offered no defence against incursion, plunder and pillage.

'Like a biscuit?' said Yadegarian.

'Wouldn't say no,' I answered.

'They're freshly baked.'

'Even better.'

The biscuit he offered me was imprinted with a

depiction of the sun rising, which I thought was most appropriate given Yadegarian's hopes and aspirations. I sat munching it in silence, then all of a sudden a fantastic idea occurred to me. During the afternoon, Hartopp had suggested that somebody might move to the unclaimed territory of the north-west. Obviously the shot was aimed squarely at Hogust, but whether it had sunk in or not was still open to question. Meanwhile, there was no reason why I shouldn't make the move myself. In fact, when I considered it properly, I realized it was a chance not to be missed. For a start, I'd be spared the unbearable sight of Thomas and Isabella emerging each morning from the shimmering white tent. Second, I could enjoy a new start with new outlooks and new horizons. Finally, I could put to the test Brigant's bold assertion that life in the north was more 'interesting'.

I decided not to mention it to the others, though. At least not yet. In the morning I'd simply pack up my tent and leave without explanation. Just for a change, it would be me who was the man of destiny, the adventurer and the pioneer. Possibly my foray into the north-west would cause a stir, but even if it did I no longer cared. All at once I felt a freedom I hadn't known since my earliest days in the field; indeed, I was so pleased with myself I almost gave the game away.

'What are you smiling about?' asked Hen.

'Nothing in particular,' I replied. 'Just pondering the future really.'

Eventually we wished Yadegarian a good evening and returned the way we'd come. Over in the south-east we could see Thomas and Isabella deep in conversation with one another. Or, more correctly, Isabella was talking to Thomas while he stood gazing vaguely into the distance. Plainly he still had a lot to learn about Isabella. I didn't know much, but I could have told him he ignored her at his peril. She had her hands on her hips (always a dangerous sign) and was addressing him earnestly on some burning issue, but he continued to pay her no attention whatsoever. Well, more fool him! If he wasn't careful he was going to lose her altogether (or so I hoped anyway).

My plan was to surprise everybody by moving at first light the following morning. When dawn came, however, it was me who got the surprise. When I looked out I saw that more tents had arrived overnight. There were nearly a dozen of them, all different colours, and they formed a second, outer circle around Thomas and Isabella. The couple were now hugely outnumbered, and it was obvious who was responsible for the influx. The new tents were very similar to those of Horsefall and Griep, with steep walls and pointed roofs, and I assumed they'd invited some friends and acquaintances of their own. Without doubt, the Great Field's fame was spreading far and wide, and deservedly so. It struck me as odd, though, that the latest contingent had chosen to arrive under cover of darkness. As I gazed at the vast array of tents billowing in the breeze, with pennants fluttering and flags flying, I wondered if this was what Isabella had envisaged all those months ago.

Still, it was no business of mine, so I began making preparations to move. I worked quickly and efficiently, sorting out my possessions and packing up my tent. Half an hour later, everything had been stowed in a portmanteau or rolled into bundles. It was going to require two or three journeys to transfer all the items to a new location, so I sat down briefly for a rest.

Over in the south-east, Horsefall and Griep were up and about amid their tents. I had no idea who was who, but I had a feeling that Horsefall was the leader and Griep his deputy. Their comportment was sober, self-controlled and dignified; they certainly weren't a disruptive element in the manner of Hogust's uproarious brigades. Even so, the way they spoke quietly with their heads together suggested there was an underlying secrecy about them. For this reason, the pair were definitely worth keeping an eye on.

They had just paused at the edge of the outer circle when Thomas appeared in his doorway and glanced all around. I could tell he was astonished by the sight that met him: he stiffened noticeably before stepping outside, then marched across to remonstrate with Horsefall and Griep. He gestured towards the new tents, jabbed at the air with his hands, and raised his voice in anger. I couldn't hear what he was saying, but the implication was very clear: by bringing in their friends, the newcomers had exceeded their welcome. Horsefall and Griep, meanwhile, seemed totally unmoved. They stood peering at Thomas with their arms folded, giving the occasional nod of acknowledgement, but saying nothing in reply. By this time, several of their comrades had emerged from their tents and begun roaming up and down the river bank. Considering they'd only been here a day, I thought they looked very much at home. Furthermore, I couldn't imagine them leaving again just because Thomas had misgivings about their presence. It was a classic predicament: Thomas now held the southeast through *force majeure*, but he was also stuck with a mighty horde on his doorstep.

The next person to surface was Isabella, and when she headed directly towards the new tents I fully expected her to join the fray. I knew from experience that she could be a fierce opponent, so I braced myself for a pitched battle. This morning, however, Isabella was cool, calm and collected; moreover, she made every attempt to resolve the impasse. For the last five minutes, Thomas had been laying down the law and getting nowhere. Isabella's approach was entirely different. She greeted Horsefall and Griep with a smile and a handshake, then listened politely as they presented their case. Again, of course, I had no idea exactly what was being said, but eventually some sort of accord was reached and the two parties went their separate ways. Whether it was settled to Thomas's satisfaction remained obscure, but at least the situation was no longer critical. One thing was certain: for the moment, he was going to have to learn to live amongst his neighbours.

By contrast, I would soon have no neighbours at all! With unbridled glee I carried my equipment to the remote north-west and set up a brand-new camp. Just as Hartopp had described, it was wild and windswept. It was also thrillingly empty. I chose a piece of ground and pitched my tent facing down the field. The south-east lay partially lost from sight beyond the turf wall, but otherwise I could see all that was going on without getting involved. It was perfect, and I kept asking myself why I hadn't made the move before.

Not until hours later did the answer occur to me. I was sitting alone by my tent and I had nobody to talk to, not even Hen. All across the field I could hear the faint ebb and flow of faraway conversations, but I was unable to join in with any of them. Apart from gazing at distant tents I hadn't really got enough to keep me occupied, and I was already beginning to regret my decision. Even so, there was no question of going back. My pride wouldn't allow such a reversal; therefore, I simply had to make the best of my new-found solitude.

As the afternoon dragged on I watched the shadows slowly lengthen, and after a while I realized I had a visitor. Plodding over the northern slope came Brigant.

'So,' he said, when he drew near, 'you've beaten Hogust to it.'

'Yes,' I replied, 'I suppose I have.'

'He proposes to move here at the first opportunity.'

'Really?'

'So he says.'

'Is he planning to sail round?' I enquired. 'Or haul his boats overland?'

'Not sure,' said Brigant. 'He hasn't gone into the details.'

This last comment came as no surprise whatsoever. The reason Hogust hadn't gone into the details was most likely because he had no intention of moving. It was all a sham. Hogust was an accomplished practitioner of rumour and speculation, and I had no doubt that he was up to some mischief or other. Still, it was nice of Brigant to bring me the latest gossip.

If only he'd waited a little longer, he would have had some proper news to tell me: news which in itself was fairly minor, yet which signalled the beginning of a gradual change in the Great Field.

It so happened that I witnessed the event without even knowing it. During the afternoon I'd spotted a lone sail moving down the river in the east, but I'd scarcely paid it any attention. I'd merely assumed it was one of Hogust's vessels on a trial run. It transpired, however, that Hollis had defied his father, borrowed a boat, and headed southward. He'd gone ashore at Isabella's former landing place and set up camp nearby. I only learnt all this the next day, and by then Hollis had been joined by his brother Eldred in a second boat. Naturally, Hartopp was thunderstruck, yet he was determined not to interfere.

'They're old enough to make up their own minds,'

he told me, when I called on him later. 'It's their choice.'

'I'm astonished they went south,' I said. 'If they were seeking uncharted territory they should have made for the north-west.'

'That's what I'd have expected,' replied Hartopp, 'but their tastes have become more refined.'

'Oh yes?'

'It seems they prefer madding crowds to wide open spaces.'

'But not their own madding crowds.'

'No,' said Hartopp, 'that would have been far too easy.'

He was plainly disheartened. He didn't utter the word 'betrayal', but he might just as well have.

To keep his mind off his many worries, Hartopp sought solace in hard work. With my assistance, he pulled his remaining boat further inland and made it secure; then he spent the afternoon clearing the rest of the nettles. I would have helped with this task as well, but there was no need. Hartopp produced a scythe from his tool store, sharpened it, and slashed relentlessly at the nettles until they all lay flat on the ground.

At the height of the operation, Hogust came sauntering along the river bank, having evidently heard the news of Hollis's flight. He observed Hartopp for some moments; then he said, 'I bet you wish you'd let me have the boats now, don't you?'

Hartopp ceased work and gave Hogust a devastating look.

'No,' he replied at length. 'I wish I'd scuppered them instead.'

Hogust said nothing more, and with a furrowed brow went wandering back the way he'd come.

Hollis and Eldred weren't the only new arrivals in the south. Over successive days, an assorted collection of stragglers, camp-followers, pedlars and importuners appeared at the crossing in dribs and drabs. Some of them found places for their tents amongst Horsefall's and Griep's; others settled on the periphery, while still others colonized the river bank. I heard of these developments via second-hand reports, mainly from Brigant. He took a great delight in relating the goings-on beyond the turf wall, especially the fact that Thomas was being slowly encircled by the incomers. Apparently, the shimmering white tent looked as if it was under siege.

'Serves him right,' Brigant remarked. 'He acts as if the whole world revolves around him, but in truth he's a mere pageant.'

'Yes,' I said. 'I couldn't agree more.'

'The way he carries on, anybody would think his tent was lined with cloth of gold!'

Brigant didn't mention how Isabella was faring in all this; perhaps he didn't know. It occurred to me that she'd probably been obliged to abandon her daily swim in the river. With all those people roaming everywhere, I imagined it was no longer possible to drift undisturbed in the dappled seclusion of the reed beds. Besides, the weather would soon be unsuitable for outdoor bathing. As each day passed, the clouds thickened and the breeze rose a little. There'd still been no rain as yet, but it couldn't be very far off.

The advent of the long, autumnal evenings coincided with another change too: it emerged that a nightly curfew had been imposed in the lower field. At ten o'clock exactly, all the lights were extinguished and the residents fell silent. Not everyone slept, however. Throughout the hours of darkness, shadowy figures could be seen patrolling the walkways between the tents, presumably ensuring that all was well. The keepers of the watch were no doubt Horsefall's men, and I wondered what was the purpose of the curfew. Quite possibly it had been arranged for Isabella's sole benefit, so that she could enjoy her slumbers uninterrupted. If so, then her influence was plainly in the ascendancy. On the other hand, the curfew might simply have been a device for maintaining law and order. This was the more likely explanation, and it was a source of profound satisfaction for the northerners, since they were free from such restrictions. Indeed, the idea of Hogust being subject to a curfew was unthinkable.

Meanwhile, the wave of migration continued apace. Fully laden boats started to appear from further upriver, and without exception they by-passed the north-eastern settlements. Instead, they headed directly for a landing stage which had recently been constructed by Hollis and Eldred. Word quickly came back to us that the pair were charging a modest fee for this service. As far as I knew it was the first occasion any kind of toll had been levied in the Great Field, and they were reputedly reaping a handsome profit from their venture. Hartopp made no comment when he heard the news, so it was hard to tell whether he was proud of his sons for their initiative, or disappointed at their blatant opportunism. Either way, the enterprise was a veritable sign of the times.

The happenings in the south-east held everyone's undivided attention. As a consequence, nobody noticed the ragged fellow who came stumbling out of the wilderness one blustery day. Like Thomas, he was bearded and barefoot, but there the similarity ended. The newcomer had no possessions and no tent; all he had was a coarse blanket which he wrapped around himself for warmth, and which he slept beneath at night. His name was Hippo, and his stated objective was to go amongst the tents and speak to the people. He chose the north-east encampment as his first port of call, and in due course presented himself at Hogust's doorway. Unfortunately, some of the longboatmen regarded this as an act of gross impudence. They seized Hippo and were on the verge of throwing him in the river when Hogust interceded on his behalf.

'Let him explain himself first,' he said. 'Then we'll decide what to do with him.'

Hippo spoke eloquently and declared that he was carrying an urgent message which he wished to impart.

'Come on then,' said Hogust. 'Let's hear it.'

'The people aren't yet ready,' replied Hippo.

'I thought you said it was urgent.'

'It is.'

'So why are you speaking in riddles?'

Hippo was clearly taxing Hogust's patience, but he seemed quite unaware of the jeopardy he was courting. Instead of answering the question, he announced loftily that first he needed to meet the people and get to know them.

'Only then can I tell my story,' he said. 'In the meantime, perhaps you'd like to contribute to the cause?'

'No, I would not!' snapped Hogust. 'If you're looking for a handout, you can go and see Hartopp!'

Accompanied by a chorus of hoots and jeers, Hippo swiftly left the camp. It was an ignoble retreat, and he could count himself fortunate to have escaped Hogust's clutches in one piece.

His arrival at the adjoining settlement, by contrast, was met with a wholehearted welcome. Just as Hogust had suggested, Hartopp proved to be a munificent benefactor. He fed and watered his guest, and even offered him the use of a spare tent. Surprisingly, though, Hippo elected to sleep under the stars.

'Until the people are ready,' he said, 'the sky will be my tent.'

True to his word, when everyone else bedded down for the night, Hippo wrapped himself in his blanket and went to sleep. (Hartopp told me later that he felt very guilty about this.)

The next morning, following a generous breakfast, Hippo resumed his mission. He meant to visit all four corners of the field, so after calling on Brigant he inevitably turned up at my door. Luckily I'd been forewarned by the others, and I was prepared for him. I listened politely as he delivered his introductory speech, which was evidently a variation on a general theme. Meanwhile, I pondered whether he was a genuine visionary, a charlatan, or merely a victim of self-delusion. For the present, I resolved to allow him the benefit of the doubt, and to treat him with civility. Therefore, when he asked for a donation, I reached into my tent and produced the biscuit which Hen had given me. For a moment I felt a tinge of regret: after all, I'd harboured ambitious plans for that biscuit. It was imprinted with the letter J, and was an integral part of my project to forge trading links between the field's many diverse settlements. Seen from this perspective, the biscuit's intrinsic worth went far beyond its face value. In the event, however, I gave it to Hippo as the price of getting rid of him.

He thanked me profusely, then said goodbye and proceeded into the south-west. His course took him past the turf wall, which he examined briefly before continuing towards Hen's tent. For some reason Hen was absent, so the next destination was Yadegarian's distant colony.

I imagined that Hippo would find Yadegarian and his companions more receptive than anybody else in the field. Like him, they were highly idealistic people, and I assumed they would embrace him with open arms. Accordingly, I was astounded when I discovered that his visit had been a complete disaster. Again I only heard second-hand reports, but it transpired that Hippo took a very dim view of the exalted copper bath. He harshly censured the settlers for polishing it morning, noon and night, condemning the practice as both 'foolish' and 'unworthy'; moreover, he enjoined them to keep the bath hidden from view and employ it only in its proper purpose. For their part, they resented his criticism and angrily drove him out of the encampment.

Hippo appeared destined forever to sleep out in the open, yet his fortunes swiftly changed when he headed for the thriving south-east quarter.

It so happened that Thomas and Isabella had recently instituted a ritual of their own. Without fail, they embarked each morning on a 'progress' through their adopted territory, following a fixed route that took them past the rows of encircling tents, then along the river bank as far as the crossing. When I learnt about this daily excursion, I concluded it was a means by which Thomas and Isabella could show themselves to the populace at large: he in his flowing white robes, she in her crimson finery. It was a calculated exercise, a further example of their unabashed regal posturing. Nevertheless, Hippo managed to turn it to his advantage. At a carefully chosen moment, he engaged with the strolling couple and urged them to beware of their own vanity. Obviously such a blunt approach carried the risk of immediate rejection; after all, Thomas was hardly renowned for his self-efface-ment and Isabella was fiery to say the least. The encounter might easily have been yet another catastrophe for Hippo, but on this occasion his luck held out. Perhaps it was the bare feet and the beard that made the difference, or maybe it was Hippo's verbal fluency. Whatever the reason, it fast became clear that Isabella found the stranger highly fasci-nating. No sooner had they met than she was entreating him to relate his untold message. Once again, however, Hippo insisted that it could not be unveiled before he had travelled to every corner of the field. This proviso served only to deepen the mystique which surrounded him, and in Isabella's case it was especially effective. At once she offered to accompany Hippo on his tour of the south-east; she also assured him that henceforth no doors would be closed in his face. Thomas, meanwhile, had lapsed into silence. It was difficult to tell if he perceived Hippo as a friend, as a potential rival, or as simply unfath-omable. At any rate, he said nothing when Isabella made her pronouncement.

Hippo's quest now rapidly gathered momentum. Escorted by Isabella, he made his way from tent to tent until the entire region was aware of his presence. He then declared that on the following day a public meeting would be held to which all were invited. Again, Isabella's assistance proved invaluable. It seemed that Hippo had privately expressed reservations about his impact north of the turf wall. He was particularly disappointed at having failed to recruit Hogust, and he questioned whether anyone from the north-east would attend the meeting. Isabella, of course, refused to countenance such doubts.

'Don't worry about Hogust,' she intoned. 'I'll deal with him.'

True to her word, Isabella marched across the field, skirted the turf wall with barely a second glance, and headed directly towards Hogust's encampment.

Poor Hogust didn't stand a chance: as a matter of fact he didn't even see her coming. He was fiddling with the sails on one of his boats, hauling them up and down the mast, when suddenly she appeared before him. This was the first time they'd met each other in person, but Isabella didn't bother with a formal introduction. Instead, she gave Hogust a severe dressing-down for the general untidiness of his camp; then, as he peered at her in speechless amazement, she issued a series of instructions concerning the time and place of the forthcoming assembly. In addition, Hogust was advised that a low turnout would not be acceptable.

'We don't want just a handful of people,' Isabella concluded. 'We want each and every one of you.'

Resistance was futile: Hogust surrendered without uttering a word.

The whole of the north now lay wide open to Isabella, and she swiftly extracted a promise of support from Hartopp.

Brigant, on the other hand, presented a far greater challenge. His list of objections was inexhaustible: they were based on an inherent mistrust of outsiders (even those approved by Isabella were under suspicion); a disdain for public meetings (because they attracted rowdy elements); and a sense of indignation at having to 'traipse' all the way to the south-east.

'Well, if you don't want to come along I can't compel you,' said Isabella, 'but it's a great shame you won't hear Hippo's story.'

'That's my lookout,' replied Brigant. 'Besides, I haven't said I'm not coming yet.'

'So there's still hope then?' she asked.

'Maybe,' he said. 'Maybe not.'

Needless to say, Isabella didn't bother summoning me to the gathering. She must have seen me standing by my tent as she made her way homeward again, but she avoided my gaze and fixed her sights on Hen instead. According to subsequent reports, he assured her that he would do his very best to attend; then he happened to enquire whether she'd be calling on Yadegarian and the other settlers in the south-west.

'Definitely not!' she snapped. 'Hippo says they're beyond redemption!'

Hen was quite shocked by the outburst, and when I met him the next day he still hadn't fully recovered.

'I only asked,' he said, in a subdued tone, 'but she practically jumped down my throat.'

He told me he still felt rather protective towards Yadegarian's people, in spite of their outlandish customs; and I confided that I felt a certain empathy with them as well.

'Sounds as if Hippo has made a deep impression on Isabella,' I remarked. 'She's not usually swayed by the judgement of others.'

'No,' said Hen.

'So I'll be intrigued to hear this story of his.'

'You're going to the meeting then?'

'Certainly,' I said. 'I haven't been officially invited, but I should be able to mingle unnoticed with the crowd.'

'Well, I'm afraid I've changed my mind,' said Hen. 'I think Hippo's going to spoil everything.'

He turned and stared gloomily into the south-west, as if contemplating some grim premonition. After a moment, however, I realized he was studying the immense black clouds which were accumulating on the horizon. I also noticed the breeze had begun to pick up a little. There was obviously a rainstorm blowing in, and it struck me as an inauspicious day to be holding a public assembly. I estimated we had two or three hours at the most, and then we'd be in for a downpour.

Not that anyone seemed remotely interested in the

weather. The meeting had been set for ten o'clock in front of the shimmering white tent, and groups of people were already starting to arrive. Hartopp and his followers initially appeared slightly cautious, but Isabella made a special point of greeting them and quickly put them at their ease. Hogust's comrades were far less diffident: noisy and disruptive as ever, they swarmed over the turf wall like an invasion force bent on conquest. Somehow, though, they managed to restrain themselves from their usual excesses, and did nothing worse than leer at the local residents. Hogust, meanwhile, had chosen to travel to the south-east by boat. He cruised down the river under full sail, and came ashore (without paying) at Hollis's landing stage. Watched closely by Horsefall's men, he strutted amongst the vast range of tents, pretending to inspect them as he passed them by. It was a cocksure display: plainly Hogust wished to put his stamp on the proceedings.

By this time I'd slipped quietly into the crowd, near the back. Beside me stood Brigant, who'd turned up at the last minute insisting he was present as a strictly neutral observer. As far as I could tell, the only absentees were Hen (for reasons of his own) and Yadegarian (who'd been explicitly banned from attending). It was quite a gathering, with numerous people packed together in a small space, and I wondered how Hippo planned to address everybody. When I craned my neck, however, I caught a glimpse of a low, wooden platform ideal for such an occasion (I later learnt that it had been built, for a fee, by Hollis). I had to admit I was impressed by the efficient organization of the meeting, and when Hippo made his entrance it was equally clear that he was very well-rehearsed.

At ten o'clock precisely a joyous cry went up, the crowd parted, and Hippo approached from the rear. The effect of an imaginary door opening before him was not lost on anybody, but the real *coup de théâtre* came when he mounted the platform. He was wrapped in his habitual coarse blanket, which he suddenly threw off to reveal that underneath he wore only a loincloth! The audience gasped; then he raised his arms for silence.

'You may not know it,' he began, 'but this is the chosen field: the place where great events unfold and come to fruition. If you take good care of it, treasure it, and act as its custodians, then you will surely reap the rewards.'

He paused to allow his words to sink in.

'But I must tell you,' he continued, 'that my people once had a field very similar to yours. It was a rich and verdant meadow; it had a river running around it; and we lived, side-by-side with our neighbours, in peace and tranquillity. We often congratulated ourselves that we had found the perfect setting, and we assumed it would last for ever.'

Hippo paused again.

'Then, without warning,' he said at length, 'the men in

185

the iron helmets arrived. They wanted the field for themselves, so they rounded us all up, destroyed all our tents,
and marched us all away.'

'Oh, how awful!' exclaimed Isabella.

She was standing at the front of the crowd, and she
clasped her hands to her face in horror. Everyone else
remained hushed, as if Hippo had cast a spell over them.
When he resumed, his voice had taken on an oratorical
quality which served only to add to the drama.

'They took us to a land begirt with pestilential marshes,'
he declared, 'and penned us in for an eternity. Our life
there was dreadful and many lost hope, but fortunately I
was able to escape. I made my way through the wilderness until I reached your bounteous pastures, where
finally I felt safe again.'

Now the crowd stirred a little, as people remembered
the day when Hippo first appeared, and how some had
treated him better than others. No doubt he'd embel-
lished parts of his story to achieve greater effect, but just
as likely it contained a substantial element of truth. There
was much murmuring amongst my fellow spectators, and
I sensed a general feeling of apprehension. Moreover, I
was rather disquieted by Hippo's reference to men in
iron helmets. Horsefall's henchmen were standing in
clusters here and there, and they'd shown no reaction
whatsoever to the remark; neither had Thomas, who was
observing the meeting from beneath his canopy.
Nonetheless, I couldn't help reflecting that a few secrets

were being kept. These, in turn, posed some unanswered questions.

In the meantime, Hippo's speech was nearing its conclusion.

'You should beware the depredations of outsiders,' he said. 'You may think that it couldn't happen here, but I assure you it's quite possible, especially if you're divided amongst yourselves.'

Now he raised his finger and pointed northward.

'That wall of turf,' he proclaimed, 'will divide and weaken you! You must tear it down at once!'

The entire crowd roared in acclamation, but at the same instant there came an even louder sound. A flash of lightning was followed immediately by the crash of thunder, and I looked up to see a vast rain cloud rolling in from the south-west. People began scattering in all directions, leaving only a handful of diehards gathered around the wooden platform.

'Quick, Hippo!' cried Isabella. 'You must get into some shelter!'

She tried to shepherd him towards the shimmering white tent, but he resisted her efforts.

'My work is not yet complete,' he said.

'Well, it'll just have to wait,' she replied. 'Come on!'

'But I can't intrude on you and Thomas.'

Heavy drops of rain were now falling everywhere. Isabella thought for a few moments, then dashed inside and returned with a neatly folded crimson bundle.

'Here,' she said briskly, 'you can have my tent.'

Before Hippo could protest she added that she was conferring it upon him as a gift, and as such it could not be declined. Under her supervision, the crimson tent was then swiftly erected by several helping-hands. It stood on the very spot where the meeting had been held, and as the rain fell it seemed to gleam in the fading light. Hippo thanked Isabella and immediately took sanctuary within.

Everybody else made for the comfort of their own tents, at which point Hogust discovered that his boat had been impounded. He paced about on the landing stage, soaking wet, and was informed by Hollis that his vessel would only be returned when he paid the outstanding fee.

'But I never carry cash,' Hogust protested. 'I don't believe in it.'

'No,' replied Hollis, 'I don't suppose you do.'

'So could you let me off just this once?'

'I'm afraid not.'

'Why?'

'Because if I let you off I'd have to let everybody else off as well,' said Hollis, 'and that wouldn't be very fair, would it?'

'Sounds fair enough to me,' said Hogust.

Despite his desperate appeals, he was getting nowhere. Hollis (who was clad from head to foot in waterproofs) refused to make any concessions, and eventually Hogust was obliged to scramble over the turf wall and scamper home on foot.

He wasn't the only one caught in the rain. My tent suddenly looked a very long way away, and as I slogged northward I noted grimly that the upper field was receiving more than its fair share of the deluge. I suppose I could have sought temporary refuge with Hen, or even Brigant, but instead I pressed on until I reached my lonely outpost. Thankfully it was dry inside, so I settled down and waited for the evening to pass. After a while I began pondering Hippo's speech, and debating whether anybody would obey his instruction to tear down the turf wall. Given the practicalities, I decided that the answer was 'probably not'. It was all very well for the multitude to applaud and cheer Hippo's commandment, but I doubted if they realized how much hard work the job entailed. This, of course, was something I knew from experience. Furthermore, they needed to understand that it wasn't simply a matter of shovelling the earth back into the trench. On the contrary, each successive layer had to be carefully tamped down flat: otherwise there'd be a surplus left over when they'd finished. Such a task required proper organization with somebody in overall charge. Obviously I had no intention of offering my services, but conceivably the challenge might be taken up by Hartopp and Hogust. Both were capable enough. Considering their previous differences, however, I concluded that the chances of a working partnership were slim.

The rain continued until the following day, and when it finally ceased there was no more gentle autumn sunshine. The sky remained grey and overcast, with a cold, damp wind blasting in from the west. Around mid-morning I went to see how the trench had coped with the downpour, and I knew at once that it had functioned most effectively. Along its entire length lay damp nettles which had been flattened by the force of the rainwater. In addition, a glance towards the south-east told me that although the ground was wet and muddy, it was far from being waterlogged. In fact, people were going about their daily business with little or no inconvenience. Apparently the drainage scheme had been a success, and it occurred to me that at last my argument was proved to be true. All the talk about divisive walls, defensive ramparts and so forth could finally be laid to rest in the name of common sense!

Or so I thought.

I was standing by the trench feeling rather pleased with myself when I heard a distant voice being raised in anger.

'Why hasn't the work begun yet?' it demanded. 'You must not delay a moment longer!'

The voice I recognized as Hippo's, and he was roaming amongst the tents rousing his supporters into action. Soon afterwards, they appeared on the embankment armed with all sorts of implements (spades, shovels, pickaxes, rakes and hoes) and started hacking at it inexpertly. I watched in dismay as large clods of earth went tumbling into the trench.

The frenzied attack was quickly joined by Hogust's men, and their approach to the job was equally amateurish. Rather than tackle it properly, they were more interested in competing with the southerners in an orgy of destruction. Laughing and joking, they swung their picks and thrust their spades into the embankment, which was now beginning to look very battered and torn. At this point Hartopp came marching along the trench. He was attempting to restore some order to the situation.

'No, no!' he shouted. 'You're doing it all wrong! You have to pack the earth down properly!'

Needless to say, his advice fell on deaf ears. Hordes of new recruits continued to arrive, seemingly intent on levelling the embankment as swiftly as possible. I noticed, however, that some were more enthusiastic than others; and that the less zealous among them had to be cajoled and prodded by Horsefall's men to make them strive harder.

My second observation was more striking. I suddenly realized that Hippo had failed to join the workforce. During the morning I'd heard him exhorting the masses to apply themselves with might and main, but thereafter he'd been conspicuous by his absence. I later discovered that he'd spent the rest of the day lounging around his newly acquired crimson tent, receiving visits from Thomas and Isabella, and generally avoiding any kind of toil.

Meanwhile, his instructions were being carried out to

the letter. The hours of relentless digging were starting to show results, and the embankment had been greatly reduced. Inevitably, though, a problem arose: the trench was almost full of excavated earth and there was nowhere to put the remainder. The only solution was to keep piling it on in the hope that it would settle down eventually. Indeed, there was no alternative. As work resumed, Hartopp stood shaking his head at the folly he was witnessing.

'It might settle down in due course,' he conceded, 'but it's likely to take centuries.'

Down at the landing stage lay an impounded long-boat. Hogust was far too proud to plead for its return, and he certainly had no intention of paying Hollis's 'extortionate fee' (as he described it). In consequence, he decided the boat could stay exactly where it was for the time being.

'I've no immediate use for it,' he remarked. 'If Hollis wants to take care of it over the winter, it's up to him.'

The news was then relayed to Hogust that his decision rendered him liable for a seasonal berthing charge. He responded by vowing never to visit the south-east again. The people down there were a bunch of sharks, he said, ready to fleece a man as soon as look at him! They could keep the damned boat and he hoped it went rotten in its bilges!

'That'll teach them a lesson!' he declared.

Hogust's portrayal of the south-east may not have been entirely accurate, but in one respect he was fairly near the truth. It seemed that every transaction was subject to some type of price, fee or charge: these were practically unavoidable, and nobody could get anything done without having to dip into their pockets. The latest swindle, apparently, was a toll for crossing the river, and it came as no surprise when I learnt that all the proceeds were going to Thomas. However, he didn't lower himself by collecting the tolls in person: instead, he appointed Horsefall and Griep as his agents. According to them, it was 'widely known' that Thomas had discovered the crossing in the first place, and therefore he was entitled to charge others for the privilege of using it.

As a matter of fact, Horsefall and Griep were playing an increasingly large part in the day-to-day affairs of the Great Field. Not only were they close associates of Thomas, but I also saw them at the landing stage talking to Hollis, and escorting Hippo when he went on his promenades among the tents. It all looked extremely cosy, and I realized that I'd slipped very much into the role of an outsider.

Horsefall's men were seldom idle, and one day they came around the field distributing handbills. They moved methodically from tent to tent, making sure that nobody was excluded. The whole task was carried out very politely, yet with an air of authority which suggested the handbills could not be ignored. I received mine just before dusk, and I sat down to read it in the twilight. It went as follows:

WE WISH TO NOTIFY EVERYONE THAT THE
COPPER BATH BELONGING TO ISABELLA WAS
MISAPPROPRIATED SEVERAL WEEKS AGO, AND
HAS SINCE BEEN PUT TO A NUMBER OF
DISHONOURABLE USES. ISABELLA DESPAIRS
AT THE LOSS OF THIS TREASURED POSSES-
SION, WHICH IS HERS BY INDEFEASIBLE RIGHT.
MOREOVER, SHE DESIRES THE BATH TO BE
HIDDEN FROM VIEW AND EMPLOYED ONLY IN
ITS PROPER PURPOSE. THOSE WHO STOLE IT
ARE BEYOND REDEMPTION, BUT THEY COULD
AT LEAST SHOW THEIR REMORSE BY RETURN-
ING IT TO ITS ORIGINAL OWNER AT ONCE.

The handbill was signed by Thomas and Isabella. I studied it closely for a few minutes to make sure I understood
it correctly, but even so I was left feeling rather bewil-
dered. Why, I wondered, had they bothered to publish a
handbill when everybody knew the precise whereabouts
of the copper bath? It was plainly visible from all four
corners of the field and was hardly a secret. If Isabella
thought she had a prior claim, then surely it would have
been much simpler to go to Yadegarian and ask for it
back. As far as I recalled, Yadegarian had taken the bath
into his custody solely for safekeeping. He was a reason-
able man, and I had no doubt that some sort of
accommodation could easily have been reached. Instead,
Thomas and Isabella were adopting this heavy-handed

approach which promised only to lead to further unpleasantness. Actually, the assertion that the bath had been stolen was quite offensive!

There was something else too. As I read and re-read the notice, I began to suspect that Hippo might have had a hand in its composition. Both the tone and the wording were familiar and, given his outspoken opinion regarding the copper bath, I became more and more convinced I was correct. Without question, Hippo's personal influence was spreading by leaps and bounds: in no time at all he'd been transformed from a ragged wanderer into the occupant of a splendid crimson tent; he enjoyed the full support of Thomas, Isabella, Horsefall and Griep; and now it seemed he was trying to turn the whole populace against Yadegarian. I peered into the descending gloom, and realized that since Hippo's arrival the Great Field had undergone yet another change.

It was difficult to tell whether anybody else shared my misgivings. The handbill was never discussed in public, but I assumed it would find little favour with the likes of Hartopp, who had a profound sense of fair play. On the rare occasions when I spoke to him, however, he made no mention of it.

I say 'rare occasions' because Hartopp was now constantly engaged in dealing with Hogust. Ever since the incident at the landing stage, Hogust had become an exceedingly difficult neighbour. He wasn't openly hostile to Hartopp, but he clearly blamed him for the way he'd been treated by Hollis and Eldred. During the following days, minor instances of sabotage started to occur around Hartopp's encampment. These were nothing serious, barely worse than ill-conceived practical jokes: guy ropes slackened, buckets of water overturned and so forth. All the same, their nuisance value soon weighed heavily on Hartopp. Obviously the finger of suspicion pointed at Hogust and his band of freebooters, who were assumed to be exacting some crude form of revenge. There was never any proof, of course, but it was generally agreed that they were behind the attacks. For his part, Hartopp quietly resigned himself to a life of unceasing watchfulness. After a while, though, a rumour began to circulate in which Yadegarian's name was linked to the sabotage. It was a blatant attempt, the rumour suggested, to sow the seeds of discord between the various settlements. I had no idea where this rumour originated, but it gradually gathered momentum until it became widely accepted as a fact. Naturally, I was outraged. I knew Yadegarian well enough to be certain he would never stoop to such measures, so I decided to raise the matter with Hen.

It transpired that the rumour had failed to reach him, but he listened with interest as I recounted what I'd heard.

'It's preposterous,' I concluded. 'Yadegarian and his companions are completely harmless. The last thing they'd do is try and stir up trouble.'

'You're quite correct,' said Hen, 'but unfortunately they're a minority, and minorities are the easiest to pick on.'

'But I'm a minority,' I said, 'and you are too.'

Hen raised his eyebrows.

'Well,' he said, 'we'd better be careful then, hadn't we?'

I pondered these words as we gazed silently at the little group of tents in the south-west.

'I don't suppose,' I said at length, 'that Yadegarian could be persuaded to return the copper bath?'

'I'm afraid not,' replied Hen. 'I've already spoken to him and he refuses to let go of it. From his standpoint the truth is plain to see: he saved an abandoned bath from vanishing into obscurity, he restored it to its original condition, and now he has the paramount claim of ownership. Furthermore, he thinks the only reason Isabella wants it back is because the weather's turned nasty and she can't bathe in the river.'

'Very well argued,' I remarked.

'And he's unlikely to change his mind,' said Hen.

It was ten o'clock in the morning: the time had arrived for Thomas and Isabella to embark on their daily 'progress'. We watched as they emerged from amid the sea of tents and headed along the river bank towards the crossing. They were all alone, which was unusual because they were normally accompanied on these excursions by Hippo, who invariably found some subject or other to discuss with the pair of them. As well as being a gifted orator he was apparently a very good listener too, and he always offered an attentive ear to Isabella. This was more than could be said about Thomas, who persisted in his habit of only half-listening. He seemed to live in a world of his own and spent many hours gazing into the distance, completely lost in thought. A sharp word from Isabella usually snapped him out of his reverie, but she still found his aloofness hugely irritating. Meanwhile, Hippo took advantage of the situation and became her trusted confidant. Thomas appeared scarcely to notice that Hippo was moving closer and closer (even his tent was next door to theirs), and showed no objection when he joined them on their strolls.

Today, however, there was no sign of Hippo, and they wandered alone. Presently they reached the crossing, where they stopped to observe Horsefall's men collecting tolls from some newcomers. Despite the deteriorating conditions, there was a perpetual flow of people travelling back and forth over the river. Thomas's Crossing (as it was now known) frequently teemed with activity, and it had become a highly lucrative source of income. All the same, I could tell Isabella was far from satisfied. Once or twice I saw her glance towards the south-west; then she turned and placed her hands on her hips before addressing Thomas. On this occasion it looked as if he was listening properly, and I guessed she was voicing her opinion about the copper bath. After a prolonged conversation, Thomas nodded his head in agreement and the two of them meandered slowly home. Down at the water's edge, the tolls continued to be levied.

'Since when has it been called Thomas's Crossing?' asked Brigant.

'The title's fairly recent,' I replied.

Brigant absorbed the information with an indignant grunt.

'Is there no limit to the man's vanity?' he enquired.

'Probably not,' I said.

I'd called in on Brigant on my way back to the north-west, and as usual we'd exchanged the latest gossip. I liked visiting Brigant because he could always be relied upon to make some disparaging comment about Thomas, a fact which I found most gratifying. Today, though, his primary interest lay elsewhere.

'This Yadegarian,' he said. 'The fellow they're all talking about.'

'Oh, yes?'

'Friend of yours, isn't he?'

'Sort of,' I said. 'We worked alongside one another for a while.'

'When you were building the turf wall?'

'Correct.'

Brigant regarded me for a few moments, then turned and peered at the ruined earthwork.

'You know, it'll never disappear,' he said. 'Not entirely.'

'No,' I answered, 'I don't expect it will.'

'There'll always be traces.'

'Yes.'

Although he would hardly admit it, I sensed that Brigant was quite pleased with this outcome. Hitherto, the turf wall had provided unarguable evidence for his concept of a divided field; moreover, it gave him a perfect excuse to rail against the iniquities of the south. If the wall had vanished completely, he would have had far less to complain about.

'Looks as if we're in for more rain,' he said, glancing at the sky. 'Perhaps not this afternoon, but definitely later, and there's going to be a lot of it.'

I left him adding yet another flysheet to his tent, and headed home. All across the field, people were battening down for the deluge which Brigant had predicted. There would be no need for a curfew tonight: as soon as dusk approached, everyone retired to their quarters and waited. The rain finally arrived around midnight, and it was much heavier than any of the previous downpours I'd witnessed. For hour after hour I listened to it hammering relentlessly on my roof, and it was still falling when daylight came.

Peering out through my doorway, I saw at once that

disaster had struck. The river was flowing in a muddy torrent and had broken its banks in several places. Wherever I looked I could see sodden ground and tents awash. Conditions were especially bad in the populous south-east, where small rivulets criss-crossed the field and caused extensive flooding. Meanwhile, down in the far south-west, Yadegarian's circle of tents had been completely flattened. Hurriedly I put on my boots and went to offer some help.

When I reached Yadegarian's encampment I heard some disturbing news. It turned out that at the height of the storm they'd suffered a raid.

'The copper bath's been stolen,' said Yadegarian, simmering with anger.

He showed me a trail in the mud where the bath had been dragged eastward.

'Who was it?' I asked.

'I don't know,' he replied. 'I didn't see the intruders, but someone said it was men in iron helmets.'

When we examined the tents we made a further discovery.

'It wasn't the storm that flattened them,' I said. 'These have been let down on purpose.'

As the rain continued falling, Yadegarian's people struggled to repair the damage. Obviously there'd been a deliberate attempt to dislodge them from their camp, and I suggested it might be wise to make a quiet and dignified departure.

'Don't be a fool!' snapped Yadegarian. 'If we leave the field now, it means they've won!'

'But what if they come back?' I asked.

'We'll worry about that when it happens!'

Yadegarian was in defiant mood, so I gave up arguing with him. Instead, we followed the trail of mud to see where it led. Unfortunately, it soon merged into the general mud surrounding the city of tents. The entire region was in chaos, and there was no indication of where the copper bath may have been taken. Yadegarian gazed at the turmoil with disdain, then marched back to assist his comrades. He declined my offer to go with him.

These days I was a comparative stranger in the south-east, so I roamed around unobserved, helping out where I could. Very soon I spotted Thomas and Isabella, who were part of a human chain conveying supplies and equipment to the worst-stricken areas. It was admirable work, and they were plainly keen to demonstrate that they were enduring the same hardship as their neighbours. I noticed, however, that the shimmering white tent remained wholly unscathed by the storm. Perhaps the stolen bath was hidden inside; perhaps not. Either way, my suspicions of the men with the iron helmets had been confirmed. The move against Yadegarian had shown just what they were capable of, and with some concern I wondered where they would turn next.

In the meantime, a huge question mark hung over Hippo. He'd played a dominant part in recent events and doubtless saw the seizure of the copper bath as a triumph. Even so, the floods had proved that he was not infallible. There was no sign of him amongst the bedraggled crowd, and I assumed he was keeping a low profile until the waters subsided. This was a wise precaution. It was Hippo, after all, who'd brought about the calamity by demanding the destruction of the turf wall. Thanks to him, an effective drainage scheme had been rendered useless, and now the consequences were there for all to see.

Oddly enough, though, the common view seemed to be quite different. As I wandered amid the debris, I began to overhear conversations about life in the early days of the Great Field. People said it was a haven of peace and tranquillity, where the grass grew in abundance, the sun shone brightly, and misfortune was unheard of. Others attested that they'd never witnessed flooding, or any other kind of catastrophe. (The majority of these claims, it should be mentioned, were made by newcomers who didn't know any better.) Soon I heard murmurings that everything had changed with the advent of the turf wall. Not only had it divided the field into opposing halves, but it had also interfered with the natural flow of rain-water. Suddenly, the floods had become a regular occurrence. The turf wall, they concluded, was the cause of all their problems; and gradually the murmurings transformed into a clamour. Hadn't Hippo warned them? And hadn't they failed him abjectly? Oh, they'd tried their best to rid themselves of the turf wall, but the men who built it had been much too clever! The wall remained barely half-destroyed, running across the field like a scar that would never fade away! Now they were stuck with it for ever, but at least they knew who the culprits were!

As the people's wrath fomented all around me, I decided I'd better make myself scarce. With this in mind, I sauntered casually away from the milling throng.

'Just a minute,' said a voice behind me. 'Where do you think you're going?'

I looked over my shoulder and saw a man approaching. He was wearing an iron helmet. I proceeded slowly for a few more paces, then stopped and allowed him to catch up.

'Well?' he asked.

'My tent's over in the north-west,' I replied. 'I'm just heading back to see if it's alright.'

'But there's work to do here,' he said. 'Everybody's supposed to help clear up the mess.'

He was a large man, with an outwardly menacing appearance, but he wasn't being particularly unfriendly. Actually, his manner was reassuringly earnest.

'I'd like to lend a hand,' I said, 'but it's pandemonium at present.'

The man peered at the enraged mob which was seething and swirling barely a stone's throw away.

'Yes, they're all rather upset,' he remarked. 'Still, they'll soon settle down now they've found someone to blame.'

'You mean for building the turf wall?' I asked.

'Of course,' he said. 'It was Yadegarian, wasn't it?'

Even as we watched, a cry went up and the crowd started surging away towards the south-west. The man in the iron helmet looked at me enquiringly, and all at once I realized I hadn't answered his question.

'Well, yes,' I said. 'That's more or less the truth.'

Magnus Mills is the author of *A Cruel Bird Came to the Nest and Looked In* and six other novels, including *The Restraint of Beasts*, which won the McKitterick Prize and was shortlisted for both the Booker Prize and the Whitbread (now the Costa) First Novel Award in 1999. His books have been translated into twenty languages. He lives in London.

A NOTE ON THE TYPE

The text of this book is set in Bembo. This type was first used in 1495 by the Venetian printer Aldus Manutius for Cardinal Bembo's *De Aetna*, and was cut for Manutius by Francesco Griffo. It was one of the types used by Claude Garamond (1480–1561) as a model for his Romain de l'Université, and so it was the forerunner of what became standard European type for the following two centuries. Its modern form follows the original types and was designed for Monotype in 1929.